TEXT

(a *Take It Off* novel)

One text can change everything.

Honor Calhoun never thought her life would ever be like the books she writes for a living. One morning while out for a run, she learns not all bad things are plots in novels. Some horrors can actually come true.

She faces off with a persistent attacker, holds her own, but in the end is taken hostage and thrown into a hole. In the middle of the woods.

But Honor didn't go down there alone.

She took her kidnapper's phone with her. With a spotty signal and a dying battery, hope is slim.

Nathan Reed is an active duty Marine stationed at a small reservist base in Pennsylvania. All he wants is a calm and uneventful duty station where he can forget the memories of his time in a war-torn country.

But a single text changes everything.

Nathan becomes Honor's only hope for survival, and he has to go against the clock, push aside his past, and take on a mission for a girl he's never met.

Both of them want freedom… but they have to survive long enough to obtain it.

TEXT

Take It Off Series

CAMBRIA HEBERT

Published by: Cambria Hebert

http://www.cambriahebert.com

Interior design and typesetting by Sharon Kay
Cover design by MAE I DESIGN
Edited by Cassie McCown
Copyright 2013 by Cambria Hebert

Paperback ISBN: 978-1-938857-33-1
eBook ISBN: 978-1-938857-34-8

DEDICATION

For Shawn.
I love you.

TEXT

"Wait for the person who pursues you, the one who will make an ordinary moment seem magical, the kind of person who brings out the best in you and makes you want to be a better person. Wait for the person who will be your best friend, the only person who will drop everything to be with you at any time no matter what the circumstances."

—Author Unknown

1

Honor

Early morning sunlight filtered through the overhead canopy of burnished autumn leaves, and crisp, chilled air brushed over my cheeks, filling my lungs with every deep inhale I took. My hot-pink Nikes pounded lightly against the gravel path on which I ran, and the sound of Macklemore filled my ears.

I loved this time of day. It was just me, the trail, and the exertion of my muscles. Running was something I knew I would always do. It was my escape. It was my way of de-stressing, of letting my mind wander wherever it wanted. I didn't have to think about deadlines, or emails, or dealing with people. I was in the moment, working my body and releasing all the tension and stress that built up inside me during the day.

I took a second to wipe my brow and then glanced up. A light breeze ruffled the trees and leaves rained down around me, littering the covered path. I could barely see the gravel because so many had

Cambria Hebert

already fallen. It was absolutely gorgeous. It motivated me to run farther, to run longer, because being out here, in the purest form of nature during the fall, was close to heaven for me.

To my right, a creek flowed, the water rushing over rocks insistently like it was racing me. Plants and trees grew along the bank, jutting into the moving water. Leaves were carried along with the current, dotting the dark water with bright spots of yellow and orange. Occasionally, a fish would jump up and splash, leaving ripples in its wake.

This trail stretched for thirty miles. Thirty miles of scenic pleasure. Thirty miles of untouched wilderness that blended in naturally with the mountainous small town where I made my home. This trail was the main reason I moved here. I felt so close to nature, so at peace. Whenever I had a bad day, I could go down to the creek or walk along the path and be instantly calmed. This place had a way of reminding me how life was bigger than just me, how I shouldn't get so caught up in the everyday that I forget to enjoy the beauty around me.

I glanced down at the pedometer strapped to my upper arm. I'd already gone over three miles. I needed to turn back. By the time I made it back to my house, I would be over six miles for the day.

Oh well. This long run earned me a big fat dessert or maybe a pizza later.

I turned and started back the way I came, toward my little house that sat right along the trail. Some spots of the path were more isolated than others. I was running along in a place that had no homes around it, but in about another mile, I would start passing a few homes and a small row of townhouses.

I rounded the bend in the path and ran over a wooden bridge that carried me atop the rushing creek and then back into the gravel. The trees and wildlife grew right up to the path here. It was dense and full. In another month or so, it would look more bare, the leaves would be mostly gone, and I would be able to see farther back into the woods. But not today. Today the plants provided ample coverage.

Unfortunately.

As I ran, something darted out from the side. I jerked, the sudden movement startling me. My stride faltered and I turned toward whatever it was, but I didn't see it.

It plowed into me, knocking me over, my hip taking the brunt of my fall. I grunted in pain and scrambled to get up.

But someone pinned me down.

I shoved at the man, and he glanced down, his eyes meeting mine. There was something cold in his blue-eyed stare. Something empty and flat.

Panic bloomed in my chest, spiking through my body as my heart rate went wild and alarm bells started sounding in my head.

Yes, I read the stories. Yes, I saw it on the news. *Woman is kidnapped. Search for missing woman continues. Woman is found beaten and dead.*

But that stuff didn't happen to *me*. That stuff happened to other people. Unfortunate women… women that weren't me.

This isn't happening to me.

A surge of adrenaline had me bringing up my knee and catching the man in his balls. He made a high-pitched sound and fell to the side. I scrambled up and took off, racing down the path, toward the road that intersected it. If I could make it there, I could flag down a car. I could find someone to help me.

The earbuds had fallen out of my ears and hung around my neck, banging into my skin and reminding me that I had my phone. My phone! As I ran, my hand fumbled, trying to yank it out of the band around my arm. Finally, I managed to grasp it and I held it up in front of me, calling up the keypad and dialing.

9-1—

He tackled me from behind and I fell face forward, the phone tumbling out of my hands, just ahead, just out of reach. I cried out and stretched my hand toward my lifeline, desperate to finish the call.

"You're going to pay for that, bitch," the gruff voice said.

I'd never known such fear in all my life. I could barely think straight. Straight-laced dread and panic took over my body, making my limbs feel heavy and numb.

Don't give in, the voice inside me screamed.

I bucked like a pony and reached forward, my hand closing over my phone. *Yes!* My joy was extremely short-lived when the man, who was still straddling my back, snatched it out of my hand and tossed it into the nearby creek.

"No," I cried, watching it swept away beneath the surface.

"No one's going to help you," the voice above intoned.

Something inside me went deadly calm. Like the fear and panic flat lined, leaving behind nothing but the sound of my deep, even breathing.

This fucker had no idea who he was dealing with.

I grabbed a handful of gravel beside my face and threw it behind me, right at the man. He didn't tumble off me, but he did swear and I felt him fidget about. I grabbed another handful and launched it at him as I pushed up on my hands and knees, forcing my way out from beneath him.

When I got to my feet, he grabbed me around the ankle and yanked me back. I reached into the hidden zippered pocket of my pants and pulled out a small container of mace. I carried it in case I ran into a bear or some aggressive animal.

I should have known that the real thing to be afraid of out here was another human being.

I flipped the little cap and depressed the button, the spray shooting forward.

But it missed him. He was still low to the ground.

Still clutching the mace, I took off running. I got maybe three steps when he tackled me again. Gravel cut into my cheek and stung my hands.

I started to scream.

I yelled as loud as I could.

He flipped me over and slapped a hand over my mouth. His face was dirty from the gravel and dust I flung at him. His eyes were no longer so empty... They were now filled with excitement.

He pressed against me. I felt his hardened erection crushed insistently against my middle, and I gagged.

He was sick. This was sick. This couldn't be happening to me.

"Shut. Up," he said and rocked against me.

I bit him.

He howled in pain and snatched away his hand. As I screamed, I reached out and grabbed at the erection that made me gag and yanked on it, twisting it, digging in my nails and hoping the pain would immobilize him enough for me to get free once more.

In the distance, a dog was barking, and I prayed that meant someone was headed this way, someone that would help me.

My attacker slapped his hand over my mouth again. The taste of blood, metallic and sharp, had me recoiling. His legs were shaking and I knew he was in pain.

But it hadn't been enough.

I saw it in his face.

I felt it in my bones.

I wasn't getting away.

I tried to buck him off one last time. I reached out for two more handfuls of gravel and dirt.

He drew back his arm and punched me. Right in the face.

And then there was nothing.

2

Nathan

I pushed away from the table, disassembled weapons covering the top, and opened up the white fridge sitting to the side of the room. The sound of hard rock filtered from the other room into where I was working. Usually I liked that music. Today it was annoying as hell.

I grabbed a Red Bull and popped the top, taking a long swig. I hoped it gave me the energy I was seriously lacking. I rolled my head around on my shoulders, working the kinks out of my neck, and then glanced back at the table.

Being tired probably wasn't the best thing when you were cleaning and assembling weapons. 'Course, I knew those guns so well I could likely do this job in my sleep. Weapons weren't just my job; they were sort of a passion and a hobby.

Weapons were also dangerous in the wrong hands.

I knew that better than anyone.

I glanced at the clock. Only a couple more hours 'til quitting time. A couple more hours 'til I was off for the entire weekend.

I was glad it was Friday. I felt like I needed a break from work, but a break from work meant endless hours to fill. I wasn't the type of man that could just sit around idle. I used to be. But not anymore. Now, I needed distraction. I needed less time to sit around and think.

Bronx walked in from the other room and snatched a Red Bull out of the fridge before turning to me. "You coming tonight?"

I grinned. "Of course. Bring your twenties. I'm feeling lucky."

Bronx shook his head. "When's the last time you actually won one of our poker games?"

Honestly, I couldn't remember. I wasn't about to admit that. I grinned. "Exactly. It's high time for me to clean yous out."

"That's a lot of talk," Bronx said, chugging the Red Bull.

"We'll see," I boasted and returned to the automatic weapon lying on the table.

"Good thing you're better with guns than you are cards," he cracked on the way out.

I chuckled. He was right. If I was as good with cards as I was with guns, I would have been able to get out of the Marine Corps a long time ago. I might even have been able to avoid some of the demons I would likely carry to my grave.

Even though I sucked at poker, I still played. Every Friday night, the boys and I got together for a weekly game. Beer, chips, sports, and cards. It was a good way to end the week—and a good waste of time.

Most Marines I knew just drank away their issues. They spent a lot of time in bars, throwing around the money they worked for all week and then waking up in some stranger's bed the next morning.

I wasn't opposed to drinking or sex.

But getting so drunk I couldn't remember my own name and having a one-night stand with someone I would likely never see again wasn't my idea of a good time. Not that I hadn't tried those things. I had. Drinking and sex was only a temporary solution, a Band-Aid over a wound. In the morning I would just wake up, the wound would still be there, and I would only feel worse about myself.

I drained the Red Bull, crushed the can in my hand, and tossed it into the trash. Flashes of last night's dream played through my head like the opening credits of an action movie. The sound of gunfire and screaming drowned out the sound of the rock music and caused me to grip the edge of the table in my hands.

My heart rate kicked up a bit and I felt a flush of sweat break out across my forehead. I took a couple deep breaths and forced away the images.

It was over.

I was in Pennsylvania now.

I was stationed at an Inspector/Instructor unit (we call it I & I) where there was no war, no violence.

I sat down in my chair as the sound of gunfire echoed through my head. "*Nate,*" a voice yelled. The sound of the explosion had me pushing back my chair and standing up, staring off into space. I knew I was

was just being haunted, but I was unable to shake the memories.

"Shit," I muttered and blinked, focusing once more on the room around me.

I stalked around the table, the thump of my boots echoing off the linoleum floor. I leaned out the doorway to where Bronx and some of the others were working. Actually, they weren't working; they were gathered around Patton's desk, looking at a magazine, all of them laughing like teenagers.

"Put that shit away!" I snapped. They all jumped like they got caught smoking weed and Patton slammed the magazine shut and slid it into his desk drawer.

"I'm going to pretend I didn't see that," I told them as they looked around nervously. Dirty magazines were a big no-no around here. Marines needed to be professional and conduct themselves like the representatives of this country they were.

"Yes, Staff Sergeant," Patton said.

"Get back to work," I ordered, and they scattered like cockroaches in a well-lit room. "And turn that music up!" I barked.

"Did he say up?" I heard one of the guys whisper to another behind me.

I strode into my office and over to the table and stared down at the stripped weapon. Maybe the methodical cleaning and detailing was exactly what I needed.

The volume of the rock music rose a notch. The loud screaming of the band shoved its way into my head.

Good.

Maybe the sound would drown out my own thoughts.

3

Honor

Consciousness worked its way into my brain like a worm wiggling into a wild apple lying beneath a tree. Little by little, reality came back. When I thought about it later, I wondered if perhaps it was my body's way of trying to protect me from what was happening.

The sensation of being dragged had awareness fully crashing over me. I felt like a tsunami swept me along, pummeling me with memories of what just happened, taunting me with whispers of the horrible fate that awaited me when I finally opened my eyes.

So I decided that opening my eyes could wait. I didn't really need to see what was happening right this second… did I? I had no doubt that whatever I would see in the very near future was going to be more than enough.

I concentrated on what was happening around me. Someone—the perverse kidnapper, I presumed—was dragging me at a fairly quick pace.

My feet and ankles were being ripped along the ground. I could feel little cuts and nicks stinging my skin near my ankles, and I bit my lip against the pain.

The man had me beneath the armpits, hauling me like a ragdoll. I wondered why he didn't just carry me; he was big enough. I wasn't a very large person (something I was seriously sorry for in that moment). All the running I did kept me thin, and I only stood about five foot three.

I was the perfect prey for someone like him.

God, I was so stupid.

What had I been thinking going out on a trail like that alone? Why hadn't I ever been scared? Why hadn't my overactive imagination cooked up scenario after scenario of all the vile things that could happen?

Maybe I should have gotten a dog. A big, mean one.

No. I didn't want that. Because if I did have a dog and he was with me today… he might have gotten hurt trying to protect me. At least I was alone and the only person that would get hurt was me.

What about your family? The spontaneous thought had tears rushing behind my closed lids. Would I ever see them again? How long would it take someone to realize I was missing? I lived a fairly reclusive life. I worked from home—I didn't have an office or coworkers expecting me at a certain time.

My family and I talked on a regular basis, but not every day. I lived alone. Sometimes I went for days without seeing anyone at all.

I could be dead by then.

My best hope was that my presence online would be noted. That someone—anyone—might notice I wasn't there posting or chatting people up like normal. But even so, my friends online wouldn't know that something was wrong. They would likely assume that I got swept up with an idea, that I was hiding in my writing cave.

Sure, after several days of not replying to messages or posting teasers on my fan page, someone would begin to wonder.

I could be dead by then.

Well, shit. I wasn't ready to die. I had a book to finish. My newest fictional boyfriend had totally stolen my heart. I couldn't let his story go unfinished.

My eyes sprang open. The will to live and stubbornness kicked in full force. I planted my feet flat on the ground and dug them in. The man towing me along faltered in his steps as my feet tried to run away.

He laughed, holding on to my biceps, and continued walking. My arms were at my sides so I whipped them up behind me and grabbed a handful of the skin on his leg and yanked. Several of his long leg hairs ripped out and the sound gave me a sick satisfaction.

"Agh!" he yelled and dropped me. My teeth slammed together when I hit the ground. I rolled onto my belly and pushed up on hands and knees. He moved fast, drawing his foot back and kicking me in the side, my ribs taking the brunt force.

I groaned and collapsed back onto the ground. The pain was searing. So sharp it made it hard to breathe. Tears blurred my vision, yet I refused to cry. I would not cry. I would not dissolve into a useless puddle.

I was going to fight.

And if I died, I was going to die trying to live.

He reached down and grabbed a handful of my sweaty hair and yanked my head back. He forced me to look into his face. I committed every detail I could to memory.

He was broad, with wide shoulders and thick biceps. His hair was a sandy color, buzzed close to his head. His thick eyebrows slashed straight above his blue eyes. His skin was olive toned, his lips thin and his jaw square.

If he wasn't kidnapping and trying to kill me, I might think he was attractive. His personality must really leave a lot to be desired if he had to resort to kidnapping women. A face like his would at least get him a date.

I wanted to ask him why he was doing this. What was his motive? What kind of sick pleasure would a man possibly get out of this? But I was afraid of the answer. Besides, I didn't need to know any of that to fight back.

"You want me to hit you again?" he growled, staring into my face.

I didn't say anything. The answer was obvious.

He jerked my hair and I cried out. Damn, that hurt. Then I bit down on my lip until I tasted blood. I would be damned if I cried out anymore. I wouldn't give him the satisfaction of seeing me in pain.

"Get up." He grunted and pulled me up. I was surprised when he drew his hand away that a huge clump of hair didn't come with it.

Anger infused me and I acted out, raking my fingernails down his nearby arm. I felt his skin give way, and I smiled. I just collected some DNA evidence underneath my finger nails.

He grabbed my arm and twisted it painfully behind my back and shoved me ahead. We walked along (more like he forced me along). I had no idea where we were. It was the woods. On top of a mountain. There were so many locations just like this one in this small Pennsylvania town that my guess would be just that: a guess.

I inhaled, the sharp scent of damp leaves invading my senses. I loved fall. Would that change? Would I forever associate this time of year with my kidnapping?

My foot caught on a branch and I stumbled. Instead of helping me, the man laughed and shoved me farther down. I fell, the side of my face hitting a small rock, and I felt the warm ooze of blood.

The man flipped me over and straddled me, sinking his bulk onto my middle. I held my breath and stared directly into his eyes, not flinching, not backing down.

"Most of 'em are sniveling and begging for their life right about now," he drawled.

Most of them?

Had he done this before? Was this like his hobby? Gross.

He ran a finger down my bleeding cheek and pulled it away, showing me the red. "You gonna beg?" he asked, sticking the finger in his mouth and sucking off the blood.

My stomach lurched.

When I didn't answer, he pulled the finger out of his mouth and planted his hands in the dirt on each side of my head. He spread his body out along the top of mine, and I fought the shivers racing up my back. His face drew closer, his hot breath spilling across my face.

"Maybe you'll like it," he whispered.

I began to struggle, to kick and hit. He grabbed my wrists and pinned them above my head and then he kissed me. It was a rough kiss, the kind that made my teeth clamp together and my jaw go solid. He ground his mouth over mine fiercely in a way that was so gross that my skin crawled. He simultaneously ground his hips against me.

I went still, playing dead. Maybe he wouldn't like a woman who lay there like a lump.

Eventually he got tired of violating my mouth and he got up, yanking me with him. He didn't drag me this time. He didn't punch or threaten me anymore. He simply picked me up like a sack of potatoes and threw me over his shoulder, making sure to keep one hand on my ass at all times.

But that was the least of my worries.

I paid attention to the ground, to the sounds around us, to the smells. I listened for traffic, for people, for anything that would help me.

All I heard was his breathing. The pounding of my heart. I felt the rush of blood draining to my head and the sharp stab of pain every time his shoulder gouged into my stomach. I don't know how long he walked. I don't know how long I'd been gone, how long I'd been passed out. The sun was higher in the sky, which told me it must have been a while.

We could be anywhere.

His steps slowed, and my entire body stiffened.

Was this it?

Were these the last moments of my life?

I noticed something then… the bulge in the back pocket of his jeans. The top of a cell phone peaked out, tempting me.

He stopped walking altogether. Silence rained upon us. Not even a bird dared make a noise. I was presented with a choice. This entire day had been nothing but a series of choices, of attempts at gaining freedom.

I lurched my body to the right, rolling off his shoulder and down his arm. He swore and threw me back up. I made an intense gagging sound, not all of it made up (his shoulder really hurt my gut). He leaned forward like he was trying to get away from a shower of puke, and my body went with him.

I flailed my arms about like I needed help, quickly making my move. Then I gagged again.

He made a disgusted sound and pulled me off him, pushed me away, and held me out. Our eyes met one final time.

And then he let go.

I braced myself for the brunt of the hard ground. Only it didn't come. My body was forced into a free-fall.

I dropped from the air, the bottom falling out of my stomach as my arms and legs searched for something—anything—to catch myself with.

But there was nothing.

The longer I fell, the darker it became. Until the sunlight was just a beacon above.

And then I hit.

My teeth banged together, biting into my tongue and filling my mouth with the tang of blood. I blinked, trying to rid my head of the throbbing, but it didn't help. I looked up… up past the tall dirt walls of my prison, up to the tiny round hole at the top.

My captor stood there staring down, watching me, not saying a word.

I lay there unmoving, feeling the damp, cold dirt at my back and against my legs. I lay there and stared at him, hoping he would think I was dead, that the fall broke my neck.

He stood there a long time.

Staring.

Watching.

Waiting.

And then he stepped away, disappearing from sight, leaving nothing above me but the image of trees and sunlight.

I lay there a little bit longer, wondering if he would come back.

When I thought it was safe, I began to wiggle my prize out of the sleeve of my running jacket, jiggling it down into the palm of my hand.

A shadow fell overhead, and I stopped breathing.

He returned.

He stared at me some more. I lay there still unmoving, gripping my lifeline in my hand. Finally, he grunted. And he said three words that scared me more than death itself.

"I'll be back."

4

Nathan

On my way home from work, I drove through the drive-thru and got a bucket of fried chicken and some biscuits. I wasn't used to being up North. When you ordered iced tea here, it didn't come sweetened. What the hell kind of person drank *un*sweetened iced tea? It was downright un-American.

As soon as the person at the window handed me the bucket and I drove away, I reached in and pulled out a leg, biting into the crispy, fried skin. It wasn't as good as they did it in the South, but it was close enough.

As I drove and ate, I marveled at the views beyond the dashboard of my Wrangler. I'd been stationed here six months, and I still wasn't used to the landscape. It was so different than what I was used to. The mountains were never ending. The way they rose right up from the ground and into the sky was remarkable.

The roads here were two-lane and curvy as hell. Driving a stick shift on these back roads was the worst. Thank God I had four-wheel drive because I had a feeling this winter was going to be a bitch.

Tall trees bursting with autumn hues filled the mountains and grew up to the roads. Rolling hills of tall grass and flowers gave way to small neighborhoods and homes perched right along the curving, dangerous roads.

Pennsylvania was a far cry from the South where I grew up. I was born and raised in Jacksonville, North Carolina. It was a Marine town if I ever saw one. The population there was probably at least half Marines. The economy was always steady because of this and there were bases scattered around town.

The land there was flat. We didn't have the mountains in Jacksonville, but there was no shortage of beaches. Because the town was so close to the coast, on a super hot day, sometimes you could smell the salt that blew in from the ocean. Jacksonville boasted two temperatures: hot and hell. Sure, sometimes it would be "chilly" in the mornings at sixty degrees, but the sun always chased away the chill.

Here in Pennsylvania, it was always cool. It didn't matter how high the sun rose, the heat could never compare to that of the South. I guess that was a welcome change. I enjoyed not sweating my balls off in my cammies all day long.

I came around a sharp bend in the road and downshifted, pulling up to my rental, which was one of those houses that sat along the winding road. It also sat away from the others, surrounded by trees and creating the privacy I desperately wanted.

The house needed some work, which was one of the reasons I rented it. It would've been easier to rent something closer to where I worked, something in Allentown. But I didn't want to be around that much congestion. I wanted room to breathe.

Plus, working on the house was a great way to keep busy. And save on rent.

I parked alongside the home and threw open the door, grabbing the chicken and biscuits and going inside.

The house was covered in wooden shingles, making it appear like it belonged in the woods, sort of like a cabin. There were overgrown bushes along the front and the yard was already blanketed with a thick layer of fall leaves.

I unlocked the chipping brown front door and walked through the living room into the kitchen. The large window over the sink flooded the room with sunlight that filtered through the trees in the back yard. I set down my dinner and headed down the hallway, unbuttoning my cammies as I went.

I peeled off the blouse and tossed it across my bed and then bent down to unlace my boots. Once those were off, I undid my boot band that held my pants in place over my boots and tossed those onto the growing pile of clothes on my mattress.

My belt and trousers were next, along with my army green T-shirt. When I was down to nothing but my boxer briefs, I went into the adjoining bath and turned on the shower. The water pressure in here sucked. But at least there was water.

Bathing with baby wipes was worse.

I peeled off the boxers and kicked them away, stepping under the lukewarm spray and pulling the curtain shut.

I stood under the water a long time, hoping it would wash away my day. But my brain wasn't going to be controlled, and it went to places I really didn't want to go.

After finishing up, I tossed on a ratty pair of jeans, a white T-shirt, and a long-sleeved thermal tee.

I sat at the kitchen counter and ate my southern dinner, the picture hanging on my fridge taunting me as I ate.

Finally, I dropped the leg I'd been working on and wiped the grease coating my fingers on a napkin. I pushed away from the stool and stalked over to stand in front of the picture, crossing my arms over my chest as if I were accepting some unspoken challenge.

The faces in that photo stared back at me, reminding me of better days, of days when I didn't carry around thick scars that no one could see.

Prior was grinning into the camera, a helmet strapped under his chin. A rifle was slung over his shoulder and war paint smeared his baby face. We used to laugh and tell him that he only wore the paint so women wouldn't think he was twelve.

To the left of Prior stood Gidding. A solid house of a man, with dark skin and a wide white smile. When he wasn't working, he was lifting weights. When he wasn't lifting weights, he was flirting it up with any pair of female legs he could find.

They were both dressed in cammies and boots, with covers perched over their regulation haircuts.

They were good men. They didn't deserve what happened to them.

My eyes wandered over the sole survivor in that photo.

Broad shoulders, narrow waist, extremely short, dark hair. The smile he wore was almost an urban legend, because it was a sight that wasn't often seen now.

He was the least likely of the trio to survive any kind of attack. He was the least likely of the trio to actually be caught in a dangerous situation.

Yet he had been.

And he was the only one who survived.

I almost didn't recognize that man in the picture, but it was hard to forget a face you looked at every day in the mirror. I looked a lot different now than I did then. Not so much in features, but in appearance. I was no longer young and motivated. I no longer carried an air of youth and innocence.

Now I was just edgy and rough. Scarred and hardened.

I gave a weary sigh.

I spent my days trying to forget. Yet I hung a reminder right on the fridge that I was forced to look at every single day.

No more.

I couldn't continue to beat myself up over the fact I was still alive.

I snatched the photo off the fridge and carried it to the trash can in the corner of the room. I stood over it a long time, staring down at the faces of my friends who were no longer alive.

Without tossing the picture away, I pivoted from the can and slid open a drawer. It was the kind of drawer that seemed to collect every odd and end in this house. MacGyver would have a field day with this thing.

I shoved the picture into the back, burying it underneath the rest of my accumulated junk that was too valuable to throw away. Then I slammed the drawer and returned to my chicken.

My eyes strayed to where the picture used to hang, my gut tightening in preparation for what it was going to see. Only the space was empty.

My gut released.

Putting that picture away wasn't going to fix my problems, but it was a start.

5

Honor

I lay there a long time, not daring to move, afraid to breathe too deeply. The earth was damp here, the moisture seeping into my clothes and making me uncomfortably cold. The sun was shining. Why was I so cold?

Because I was in a hole.

Because I was kidnapped and thrown down some sort of manmade pit. I began to wonder how he dug such a hole, how long it took and if he only used a shovel. How did he get out when he finished digging?

Was I going to get out?

A little whimper escaped my throat and it seemed to snap me back to reality. He was gone; it was clear he would be gone a while. My fingers, now freezing cold and super stiff, ached from clutching my possession.

The one I stole.

I lifted my arm, holding it up. It was an iPhone. A little smile played over my lips. He'd been so busy worrying I would puke on him that he didn't notice my little pickpocket scheme. I wondered how long until he realized it was missing, how much longer after that it would take him to check back here.

My time was limited. I had to act fast.

I pressed the circular button at the bottom of the screen and the phone lit up. It was the afternoon. By now, I would have been showered, dressed in a comfy pair of yoga pants and an oversized sweater, with a cup of coffee steaming at my elbow while I typed away at the kitchen table.

I pushed away the images of my cozy, serene house. I pushed away the panic budding inside me. I was going to get out of this. And once I did, I would have new material to write about.

The screensaver on the phone was generic and plain. A simple blue background that made me roll my eyes. Did he have no creativity at all? I swallowed thickly. Obviously he had some creativity because I was lying in a hole that had to be over thirty feet deep.

The battery on the phone was at seventy percent, and I sent a small prayer of thanks that it wasn't almost dead. I pressed the small green square that said PHONE and called up the keypad to dial for help.

Quickly I punched in 9-1-1 and then held the phone to my ear with a shaking hand.

Nothing happened.

After a very long time, I pulled the phone away from my ear and stared at it. No signal.

"Are you freaking kidding me!" I yelled. What the hell was the point of a cell phone if you couldn't use it when you desperately needed to?

"Oh, hell no," I muttered and hit END.

I sat up, my stiff, cold body screaming in pain. I ignored the intense ache in my ribs, ignored how it hurt to breathe. I ignored the way my cheek stung and my tongue felt thick. I pushed to my feet, using the dirt wall to steady myself, and then blinked at my surroundings.

I looked down at the phone and went to the home screen, hoping there was a flashlight app. There was so I used it, shining it around the hole. It was maybe ten feet wide. The floor was uneven, all dirt, and the sides were the same. The sky seemed so far away when I looked up.

My vision was blurred, and at first I thought tears were threatening again, but they weren't. After several minutes of really taking stock of my body, I realized only one eye was blurry—because it was swelling shut. Likely from where he punched me.

Well, on the bright side, I didn't have to worry about the way I looked because no one could see me.

A hysterical laugh bubbled out of my throat and I swallowed it, returning my attention to the hole. I studied the ground, the walls, everything. I wanted to know everything about this pit I now called home.

As I was shining around the flashlight, something glinted in the side. I stepped closer, bending down to look. It was a necklace. A silver locket with a red stone set in the center. Around the stone was a beautiful engraved scroll design. I picked it up, brushing away some of the dirt caked on it. The metal was cold and I knew instinctively that it had been here a while.

I also knew I hadn't been the first woman to be thrown down here. I stared at the necklace a long time. I didn't really see it, though. Every ache and pain in my body became more pronounced. My knees shook with the cold and my teeth began to chatter. I knew that I was likely going into shock and I told myself to calm down. The only way I was going to get out of this was with a clear head.

I tucked the necklace in my jacket pocket, not willing to put it back in the dirt, and I prayed whatever poor woman had lost it here was somewhere at peace.

I also made that woman a vow.

Justice.

Justice for what was done to her. Justice for her life, though way too short. I knew she was dead. He wouldn't keep kidnapping if she wasn't. I hoped her end was swift.

I tried 9-1-1 again. I paced around the circle, trying to find a signal, waiting for just one call to go through.

Finally, the dial tone came on and the phone rang in my ear. Excitement and hope flooded me, and I sagged in relief. Then the phone beeped. The ringing stopped. The dial tone went away. I looked at the screen.

Dropped call.

I sank down onto the ground. I was so utterly exhausted. My eyes felt like they had a ton of sand in them. I leaned against the dirt wall, tucking my legs beneath me, gathering myself close, trying to keep in my body heat.

I would just rest for a minute and then I would try the phone again. The second I had even a smidge of a signal, I was going to get someone on the line. I was going to tell them what happened and they would come for me. I would be safe.

Even as my eyes drooped, I tried the phone again. The call didn't go through.

I was still attempting the call when my body succumbed to my exhaustion and I fell into a troubled and painful sleep.

6

Nathan

I needed a beer. There was no beer. And why was there no beer at this weekly poker game?

Because the dude bringing it was late.

I'm pretty sure that somewhere written in the guy code of life was a rule that stated, "He who brings the beer shows up on time."

Clearly this guy needed a class on guy code.

"Where the hell is the beer?" Patton complained as he shuffled the deck for, like, the thirtieth time.

"I say we dock him a hundred in chips when he gets here," Braden said.

"There's liquor behind the bar," Jinx, our host, said, getting up and going around the wooden bar against the wall. "Who wants a drink?"

A couple of the guys yelled out their orders and a few more made jokes about leaving and going to Twin Peaks (it was like Hooters) for their drinks.

I stayed quiet. I didn't want liquor. I wanted beer. Beer was good for mellowing the mood, and for some reason I wasn't feeling too mellow. I thought finally taking down that picture, finally resolving that it was time to move on, would give me a sense of peace.

But I didn't feel any peace.

Instead, I felt kind of edgy, kind of keyed up. It was as if something was happening around me that I didn't know about, yet I could feel the bad energy.

Yeah, like I said, I seriously needed that beer.

"Should we just start the game? Make him sit out the first hand?" Patton said, returning to the chair beside mine with what looked like Captain Morgan and Coke in his hand.

"You driving?" I drawled, giving the glass a pointed stare. Yeah, I sounded like an old man, but he was one of mine. I wasn't about to let one of mine screw up his life over a couple drinks.

"I'm crashing on the couch," he replied.

I nodded and let the subject drop. I wasn't a nag and I took him at his word. Besides, he knew I would come down on him if he got behind the wheel of his car. Marines were never really "off duty." Marines were on call twenty-four seven.

Acting like an ass wasn't part of the job.

Patton started dealing the cards, and I glanced at the door once more. I wasn't what I would consider friends with the guy bringing the beer. Lex was more or less and acquaintance that I saw every Friday at our poker games. I knew him well enough that if I saw him out in town or at a restaurant, I would stop and say hi, maybe make a few cracks about poker or something. But he wasn't someone I would go watch a game with either.

I fished my cell out of my pocket and called up his name in my contacts. All of the regular poker players exchanged numbers a while back, in case of a location change or if something came up and someone couldn't be there. It was common courtesy to let the others know because we usually held up the game until we were all around the table.

Which made his tardiness that much more peculiar.

"Anyone hear from Lex?" I asked. Maybe he wasn't coming.

No one spoke up; everyone shrugged. "It's not like him to be late," one of the guys said as he adjusted his chips into neat stacks.

"Shit comes up," Jinx said matter-of-factly, sitting down with a huge ass glass of some kind of liquor concoction.

Bottom's up, I told him silently. The faster he got hammered, the faster I would start winning. I hadn't lied when I told Patton I was feeling lucky.

I fully intended to walk away with full pockets tonight.

I hit the message button and shot off a quick text to Lex.

You're late. U coming?

Hopefully he would reply with a yes or no and we could get on with the game. And someone could make a damn beer run.

How Jinx could have that bar and no beer was beyond me. 'Course, last weekend we were all here watching football so I guess I kind of knew where the beer had gone.

I dumped the phone in my lap and picked up my cards as the game began. I grabbed up a handful of peanuts and tossed them into my mouth, crunching away as I studied my cards. Not a completely worthless hand. I could work with this.

A few minutes later, the basement door opened and Lex came into the room carrying two paper sacks, which he set on top of the bar. A series of "heys" and "what ups" sounded around the room.

"Beer's here!" Patton called and elbowed me.

I grinned and laid my cards facedown on the table. "No peaking," I told him.

He snorted and started talking smack. "Please. Your mom could play a better hand than you."

I grinned because he was right.

Lex was pulling out a case of Miller Light from the bag as I approached. "Thanks, man," I said, reaching in to grab one.

"Sorry I'm late. Traffic was a bitch and the liquor store was packed."

"No worries," I said, popping the top and letting the beer flood my mouth. *Ahhhhh.*

Lex grabbed a beer and chugged about half the can in one gulp. I eyed him. He seemed a little fidgety, not quite as steady as he usually was. He was usually more friendly, more prone to smile.

"Everything okay?" I asked him.

"Hmm?" he said, pulling the beer away from his lips. "Yeah, totally. Long day at work is all."

"I hear that," I said and saluted him with my beer. "TGIF."

Lex grinned. "Deal me in!" he called, and then we both went over to the table to start the game.

I completely forgot about the text I sent him...

Until a few moments later when I got a reply.

Honor

The sound of beeping woke me. I jerked awake, blinking against the dark as reality came crashing over me. I scrambled to my feet, looking up toward the top of the hole. The sun was no longer in the sky. It was dark. It was night. I was in the center of the woods.

Even down in this hole, I could hear the wildlife singing in the night. I heard the rustling of leaves and wondered what was up there, praying it wasn't *him*.

The beeping sound cut through the darkness again, and I noticed how the screen on the phone illuminated the hole, casting a bluish tone over everything.

It was a text.

My knees sagged in relief, and I felt my lower lip wobble. Finally, I would be able to get help. I glanced at the screen, hungry for contact with the outside world. There was no name for the person texting, only a number. The area code was one I didn't recognize.

You're late. U coming?

I had no idea what kind of person my kidnapper could be friends with, but right about now I'd take my chances with anyone.

Please help me.

The signal was still very low and it took the text forever to send. It took so long that I began to lose hope. I began to think it wouldn't go through. But then the phone made a little whooshing sound and the message posted.

It took even longer for the person to reply than it did for the message to send. I waited, clutching the phone, praying I would get an answer.

What's wrong? Shitty hand?

I was kidnapped by the owner of this phone. Plz help me. Call 911.

That's a sick joke.

I'm not jkin! I swear! I typed furiously. My stomach churned. What if this person thought I was just pulling a prank? What if they thought the man who owned this phone was being funny.

I swiped an angry tear off my cheek and cleared out of the texting screen to pull up the keypad and dial 9-1-1. The phone rang.

"9-1-1, what's your emergency?" said a calm voice over the line.

I gasped, so grateful it worked.

"State your emergency."

"My name is Honor Calhoun. I've been kidnapped. I'm being held against my will."

"What is your location?"

I'm sorry, but I was offended. She didn't gasp in outrage. She didn't ask me if I was okay. She was like a damn robot on the other end of the line, asking me to take some stupid survey about orange juice or vitamins.

Hell-O! I wanted to scream. *Do you have any idea what I've been through?*

But I didn't. Instead, I replied, "I have no idea. I'm in the woods. In a hole in the ground."

The operator paused. I figured that was the biggest "Oh shit!" reaction I was going to get. I could hear her clicking away on a computer and I imagined her assembling the cavalry, riling the troops.

Go save Honor!

I'm a writer. I'm dramatic. Let's all move on.

"Stay on the line while we try to locate your phone," the woman said. Clearly, she never wrote a thing. She probably didn't even like to read.

Ring. Ring.

Hello?

I've been kidnapped. Someone wants to kill me!

Hold please.

I'd get better service at McDonald's.

"Listen to me," I said, ignoring her. "I'm in the woods. I'm scared. My name is Honor Calhoun. I live on Main Street in Slatington. Please come find me. Send help."

"Hello?" the operator said. For the first time, emotion showed in her voice. "Ar… you… th…?" Her words broke up, the connection failing.

I gripped the phone tightly, suddenly sorry I made fun of her voice. She was the only one who could help me.

"Please," I whispered, my voice cracking.

"We'll do every…. we can—" the woman said, but her words were cut off when the phone lost its signal.

I groaned in frustration and pulled the phone away from my ear. I glanced down. Less than half the battery remained.

I thought about calling back. I knew it would probably be useless. Maybe in a few minutes whatever signal was out there would come back. Maybe she heard enough of what I said. Hopefully she got my name. She wouldn't forget about me. It was her job to help.

Right?

If I couldn't depend on someone else, then it was up to me to get myself out of here. I tucked the phone into the pocket of my jacket and looked up. The sky was utterly dark. With all the trees above, I couldn't even see the moon or any stars. I could barely see two inches in front of me.

Waiting until morning to at least try to get out of here wasn't an option.

I walked over to the wall and laid my palm against the loose, moist dirt. It crumbled slightly beneath my touch. I pushed harder against it, satisfied when it packed down. Using the toe of my right foot, I drove it into the side, kicking a little, trying to delve my foot in and catch hold. When part of my foot was solidly encased in dirt, I reached above my head and forced my fingers into the earth.

I started to climb.

I took my left foot and brought it up, trying to drive it into the side just a little higher than the right. It was more difficult than I hoped. I fell several times.

Each time I got a little more desperate; each time I got a little more tired.

Eventually, I made it a little ways off the ground. My arms and shoulders trembled with exhaustion. I felt as if I'd just carried about fifty pounds worth of groceries up three flights of stairs and across a living room.

I paused in my efforts and leaned my forehead against the wall. The earthy smell of dirt washed over me. It was strong and outdoorsy. Any other time, I might have thought it was pleasant.

Now it reeked of death.

The phone in my pocket beeped and startled me. I let out a little shriek and jerked, falling off the wall and tumbling onto the ground, landing on my back.

I sucked in a sharp breath, which caused even more piercing pain than I already felt. My side ached. It felt swollen and uncomfortable, and I just wanted to lie there and cry.

I allowed myself a few long seconds to brush the sweat and dirt off my face. The phone beeped again and I pulled it out and held it above me, staring up at the lit-up screen.

I couldn't understand why sometimes the stupid thing worked and sometimes it didn't. This guy seriously needed a new cell provider. Of course, I would rather it only work a little than not work at all.

Prove it, the text read. I couldn't even be angry by the request. If I suddenly got a text from someone claiming to be kidnapped, I would probably want proof too.

I cleared out of the messaging screen and pressed the camera button.

If he wanted proof, I'd give it to him.

After making sure the flash was on, I held the phone out away from my face. Right before I snapped the selfie, I grabbed the locket out of my pocket and held it up beside my cheek. I don't know why. It just felt like the right thing to do.

I snapped the picture and then pulled the phone down to view it.

I grimaced. I looked like hell. I looked worse than hell. I looked like something that crawled out of a grave on some B-rated horror movie.

The bottom fell out of my stomach. What I was experiencing right now could *totally* be part of a horrible B-rated movie.

The entire picture was cast in that yellow-ish kind of glow that a flash provides. My face was streaked with dirt. My skin was pale, my eye was completely swollen and dark, my lips were caked with dried blood, and my hair was half falling out of its pony. Beside me, the necklace was clear, and I nodded, thinking that was good.

I sent the person my photo.

If that wasn't enough to get some help, then nothing would be.

The picture failed to send twice. The little red exclamation point beside it drove me mad with desperation. By the time it went through on the third try, I'd bitten down three of my fingernails until they were bleeding.

It was cold down here. Parts of my body began to go numb, and I huddled against the wall, pulling my knees in as far as my side would allow, and then wrapped my arms around them. I rocked back and forth, trying to create warmth.

Trying to create comfort.

I was watching the screen when I got another text.

What's your name?

Honor Calhoun. *Please, God, let this person believe me. Let them help me.*

I'm going to get you out of there, Honor.

I started to cry. I said I wasn't going to cry. I said I wouldn't give my kidnapper the satisfaction. This wasn't about that.

This was about the hope that burst through me. This was about the possibility of me actually living to see tomorrow. This was about another human being who was going to make sure I wasn't alone.

I'm scared, I texted.

I know. We're going to figure this out.

What's your name? I needed to know. I needed something to hold on to. Something to whisper in the dark of the night.

Nathan.

I gripped the phone tightly.

There was now something standing between me and absolute death.

His name was Nathan.

8

Nathan

Someone beat her. Someone used their hands—their fists—as weapons to inflict pain on her. She was small. I don't know why her slight frame bothered me so much. Maybe it was because it didn't match the determination, the absolute stubbornness buried deep in her icy blue eyes.

I laid the phone in my lap and looked across the table at the man whose phone I was getting texts from. At first I thought he was playing a prank. But I watched him. He wasn't holding a phone. He didn't occasionally glance down at his lap like it was lying there. Lex's hands remained above the table on his cards at all times.

He didn't look like the kind of man that would kidnap a woman, beat her, dump her in the center of the woods, and then drive to a poker game and have beer with the boys.

Yeah, and everyone thought Ted Bundy was nice.

He caught me looking at him and I forced myself to smile. "You gonna fold or raise?" I said, pretending like I was only looking at him because of the game.

He smiled and took a pull of beer. "I'll raise," he said confidently and threw some chips in the center of the table. I didn't even pay attention to how much he threw in.

How could someone just sit there and act like they didn't have some hideous secret? How could he sit there and act like he wasn't worth the scum on my shoe?

Questions like that usually had no answers. Answers a sane man wouldn't understand. I learned a long time ago, in the center of a warzone, that actions spoke louder than words. A man could open his mouth and spew forth a bunch of pretty lies and no one would think twice, yet that same man would then come back hours later with machine guns and homemade bombs and totally obliterate the ones he fooled just hours before.

I learned the hard way not to trust outward appearances.

I glanced back down at the phone hidden in my lap. The screen had gone dark. But it didn't matter. Her image—her face—was seared in my brain.

Dark, tangled hair, blue eyes, one of them swollen shut, a bloody lip, and huddling against a very dark backdrop. It was almost like she was sitting in the center of a vast pit of nothing— waiting for its chance to swallow her whole.

Something about that image—about her face— haunted me. It stirred up feelings deep in my gut that I didn't expect.

Could I trust her appearance?

Could I trust that text? Was it some sort of sick game? A trick?

"Nate," the man on my right said. "In or out?"

I glanced at the cards in my hand. I had a royal straight flush. I could take this game. I could have all the money piled in the center.

"Fold," I said, shaking my head like I was mad at my lousy hand. I didn't have time for this and I didn't want the attention of winning. Not here. Not right now. I hadn't been wrong when I said I was lucky tonight, except now it seemed luck wasn't the only thing I had tonight.

One of my buddies clapped me on the back. I grunted and pushed away from the table, tucking my phone in my back pocket. "I need another beer after that shitty hand."

As the game continued, I walked toward the small wooden bar. I pulled out another Miller Light and looked up. Above the bar was a medium-sized flat screen showing sport highlights. The coverage clicked off and a news bulletin crossed the screen.

The search for twenty-one-year-old Mary Greenberg is still underway. There have been no new leads or sightings since she was reported missing just over one month ago.

A picture of a blond-haired woman with brown eyes and an innocent smile flashed onto the screen. My eyes went right to the image and got stuck there.

It wasn't her face that held me captive.

It was what was hanging around her neck—a locket with a red gem in the center.

The girl in the picture on my phone was holding up a necklace exactly like the one on the TV screen.

What were the odds they would both have identical necklaces?

Two missing girls, one necklace.

There was something else I learned during my time at war. There were no coincidences.

I turned away from the TV and leaned against the bar, pretending interest in the card game. Casually, I pulled out my phone and called up the photo, staring hard at her image.

What's your name? I finally texted. I needed a name to go with her face. It didn't seem right that someone could affect me so much when I didn't even know her name.

Honor Calhoun.

Honor. I liked that name. It was strong. It was unexpected. I wasn't going to ignore those texts. I couldn't. If I did, it would haunt me for the rest of my life. I didn't need anymore ghosts.

I'm going to get you out of there, Honor.

It was a promise. It was a vow. I never broke a promise. And I never left a man (or woman) behind.

I'm scared.

Those two words did something to me. She could have said a million other things. But she chose those two words. Two words that made her even more vulnerable than clearly she already was. I swallowed past the lump in my throat as my fingers moved over the keypad.

I know. We're going to figure this out.
What's your name?
Nathan.

Someone at the table whooped with joy, and I heard the sliding of a pile of chips across the table. It was Lex. I felt my lip curl in contempt as my body filled up with suppressed rage and adrenaline. I could just beat her location out of him.

I had ways of persuasion that would surely work.

But something inside me whispered to hold back. That a beating was letting this sicko off easy. If what I suspected was true, then he hadn't just kidnapped one woman, but at least two… and if he did it twice, I had no doubt there was a string of violated and dead bodies behind him and plans for more in the future.

This guy deserved something far worse than just a beating.

Besides, Honor had been stuck God knows where for God knows how long. She was probably cold and hungry, and from the looks of her, I knew she was injured.

I set the still full beer on the bar and tucked my phone into my pocket. "Sorry, guys, I gotta head out."

"So soon?" one of the guys said, glancing at me.

"Yeah, someone from work texted me, needed me to fill in for duty tomorrow all day." I lied. I didn't have to stand duty for another two weeks.

"That sucks."

"You're telling me," I drawled. That wasn't a lie. Duty sucked. I had to go sit at the desk all day and night, do patrols around the facility, and answer the phone in case messages came down and needed to be passed to the higher ranks I worked with. It was boring. It was endless. It was part of the job.

"Gotta go get my beauty sleep," I cracked. "I'll see you next week? Same time, same place?" I asked, stopping beside the table and glancing at Lex.

"Absolutely, man," replied Patton. He was the one who introduced me to these weekly poker games. I was starting to rethink my decision of ever coming.

"Just don't let Lex bring the beer next time. We need that shit on time," I said, grinning at Lex. I hoped it looked more friendly than I felt.

Lex grunted. "A guy runs late *one* time," he muttered while he dealt a new hand of cards to everyone at the table. All the guys laughed.

"I sent you a text, man. Did you get it?" I said, watching closely for his reaction. I hadn't seen his phone in his hands all night. Now I knew why. Part of me hoped he would pull it out of his pocket and check it for the missed message. Part of me hoped I really was wrong about what I was thinking. I couldn't think of anyone who would want to be right.

He made a face, like he didn't know what I was talking about. He reached around to his back pocket where I assumed he sought out his phone. I watched the alarm pass through his eyes as he patted his pockets a little more furiously.

Interesting.

He stood and reached into the front pocket of his jeans. They were empty too. His eyes flashed up, meeting mine. I recognized the look that lay deep within. Panic and fear.

Well, shit. If that wasn't guilt, then I wasn't a Marine. A little surge of unease rippled through me. Would he know Honor had it? Would he leave here and go seek her out? Would he punish her for what I said?

Maybe I should have said nothing at all.

But I had to be sure... I had to be sure that this fucker really was guilty as sin.

And now I knew.

I forced myself to smile, not wanting to let on that I suspected a thing. "Probably fell out of your pocket on the way over here. It's probably in your car."

He relaxed, a relieved look crossing his features. "Yeah, probably."

"My damn phone is always disappearing on me. Too bad it hadn't disappeared tonight before I got called in to stand duty."

Lex laughed. "Yeah, I think I'll enjoy my break without it and look for it later."

I offered him the beer I hadn't even bothered to take a sip of. "Refill?"

He took it and smiled. "Hell, yeah."

After a few jokes, I made my way out of the house and walked toward my Wrangler. It was olive green with a black top.

I sat in the dark inside my Jeep for several minutes, making sure that Lex hadn't been faking his relief, making sure he didn't rush out into the driveway to search his truck for his phone.

As I waited, I called up the picture on my phone once more and stared down at the photo. Even beaten and scared, she was beautiful.

Once I was sure Lex wasn't going to be rushing away from the poker game, I fired up the Jeep's engine.

Give me all the details about where you are, I texted and slid the phone into a cup holder behind the gear shift.

I knew it would likely take a few minutes for her to reply. She must be somewhere with a shitty signal. I put the Jeep in gear and pulled out onto the road.

I had somewhere to be.

9

Honor

He threw me in a hole in the woods, I texted, desperately searching my brain for any kind of detail that would help save my life.

In the dark of the hole, I crouched, gripping the phone like it was my entire universe and desperately awaiting Nathan's reply.

None came.

I brought up the screen and peered down at the message. It had a red exclamation point beside it. The message hadn't sent.

"Damn it!" I yelled, pissed at the shitty cell service. Pissed at being tossed into a hole like yesterday's garbage.

My entire body hurt, my fingers and toes had gone numb from the cold, and a different type of exhaustion was beginning to cloak my entire body. I knew I couldn't surrender. I knew I had to fight.

Why did fighting have to be so damn hard?

I forced myself to stand up, to walk around the small hole, sticking close to the sides and walking in circles. I was like a hamster running on a wheel but never getting anywhere.

I needed to generate all the warmth I could. Thankfully, it wasn't winter, but it was fall, and at night the temperatures here dropped. I was only wearing a pair of spandex running capris, sneakers (with socks), a white Under Armour T-shirt, and a fitted hot-pink jacket.

It wasn't enough protection against the elements at night or trapped in a damp hole. As I walked, I pulled out the phone and glanced at the screen. The battery was still less than half, but at least it wasn't dangerously close to dying. I kept my eye on the signal bars as I moved, hoping I would eventually move into a spot where there was something I could use.

About ten minutes later, one lone bar appeared.

I stopped walking and kept my feet planted on the ground. I didn't bother to shoot off another text, not just yet. Instead, I redialed 9-1-1.

The phone rang.

"9-1-1, please state your emergency."

I sagged in relief. "My name is Honor Calhoun. I was kidnapped. I'm being held in the woods."

The woman started to talk and then line went dead.

I screamed, my throat feeling raw and the force of my yell causing pain in my ribs. Tears blurred my vision, but it didn't matter. I didn't need to see down here. I was trapped, alone, in nothing but a dirt hole where I was to await some hideous fate.

Had my luck with the phone run out? As the night wore on, would the darkness chase away the slim signal I'd been clinging to since I pulled out this phone?

Dread was a hard knot that settled in the pit of my stomach. I glanced at it again. Still no signal. I thought about Nathan. About where he was. If he thought I was dead because I never replied, would he give up on me?

Dear God, don't let him give up.

10

Nathan

The inside of the police station was like a ghost town. It seemed odd that they would have such a skeleton crew working on a Friday night.

I rushed in the set of front double doors, expecting to be greeted with noise and uniforms, with concerned faces and a staff of support ready to help me find Honor and bring down that sick bastard Lex.

I wasn't expecting to be met with a bunch of ringing phones and a couple of secretaries sitting behind desks cluttered with paper.

One of the women perked up when she saw me stop behind the chest-high counter between us. She got up from her desk and hurried forward, her blue dress swishing around her ankles as she moved.

"Can I help you, sir?"

"I need to report a missing person."

She pulled out a stack of forms and a clipboard. "When's the last time you saw the missing person?"

"I've never met her."

That earned me an odd look. The woman lowered the clipboard. "You want to report a missing person that you've never met?" I nodded and opened my mouth to explain further. She got this pinched look on her face. "I don't have time for pranks, young man."

"This isn't a prank. I have proof. And I'm pretty sure she was kidnapped."

For some reason, that statement didn't seem to warrant any kind of urgency. Frankly, I found it offensive. I opened my mouth to tell her exactly what I wanted her to do when she thrust the clipboard, bursting with papers, in front of me.

"Here, go sit down. Fill these out. Someone will be with you when they can."

"This is an urgent matter," I said.

"As soon as someone gets back, they will help you."

"Gets back from where?"

She sighed, exasperated. "There was a massive pileup over on Route 210. Mass casualties. All our personnel have responded."

"How long ago was this?" I asked, thinking that might be the traffic Lex said held him up on his way to poker.

"About an hour ago, maybe a little more." The phone on her desk started ringing and she gave me a look before rushing off to answer it. I glanced at the other woman behind a desk. She was on the phone too, writing something down.

A feeling of dread formed in the pit of my stomach. An accident with mass casualties could keep the station here busy all night. I sat down in one of the black, uncomfortable chairs against the wall and glanced at the papers in my hand.

Name of missing person. Address of missing person. Date of birth. Address. Last known location. Description.

I swore under my breath. The only thing I knew was her name. I didn't know any of this. The only way I was going to get someone to take me seriously was to show them the texts on my phone.

I glanced down at the dark screen.

She hadn't replied to my last text. I wondered if she even got it.

I need to know where you are, I typed out.

I sat there for a long time, waiting for an officer to come and help, waiting for a reply from Honor.

I'm in the woods. In a hole. My phone buzzed with her reply. I felt immediate relief because at least the lines of communication were still open… at least she wasn't dead.

Where?

Not sure. I was in Slatington when he took me. On the trail.

I wasn't that far from Slatington now. I could go and look around. Unfortunately, there were mountains and woods all over this part of the state. The trail in Slatington ran for thirty miles. I could veer off the trail to look in the wooded areas, but that was a lot of ground to cover.

But it was a start.

Do you have GPS? I texted back.

Several long moments later, I got her answer. **Yes.**

I stood up abruptly and laid the clipboard in the now empty seat, and I headed for the door. I heard the secretary call out behind me, but I didn't stop.

Screw waiting for help.

I was a United States Marine.

I was the help.

I climbed into my Jeep and fired up the engine.

This is what I want you to do… I texted and then started to drive.

11

Honor

I walked forever it seemed. Looping around the hole until there was a definite path in the crudely dug ground. Hope was a strong emotion, but it was fleeting.

How incredibly hard it was to hold on to when it seemed that everything was working against me. The words of my kidnapper seemed to echo in the enclosed space around me.

I'll be back.

What kind of grim fate awaited me when he returned? The writer in me conjured up all sorts of scenarios—not one of them good.

I didn't want to admit it to myself, but I knew what was coming. I knew the kinds of things that a man who kidnapped women wanted. I shuddered and leaned against the damp, muddy wall. I should prepare myself.

How did one prepare herself for rape and grisly murder?

Just when despair seemed ready to take a giant bite of my sanity, the phone buzzed.

I need to know where you are.

It was Nathan. He hadn't forgotten about me. He was still out there; he was still trying to help me.

I sank down the wall until I was sitting on the ground. My body sagged, weak with relief. Nathan was my best hope for survival.

Renewed hope took root inside me and blossomed like a flower in the spring.

Quickly, I texted back my reply. **I'm in the woods. In a hole.** If I wasn't so exhausted, I would have done a happy dance when it went through.

Where?

Not sure. I was in Slatington when he took me. On the trail. I worried that it wasn't going to be enough information for him to find me in time.

Do you have GPS?

A GPS? Did he think I just walked around with one of those strapped to my ass? God! I cleared out of the message, frustrated, and stared down at the phone. My eye went right to the maps app. Oh my God, I *did* have a GPS!

I pumped my fist in the air. I didn't even care that it made my ribs scream.

Yes, I replied.

This is what I want you to do...

It took a few more minutes for the rest of his message to come through, and my stomach knotted as I thought I'd lost the connection again. But then the phone vibrated in my hand and I glanced down.

Type in directions. Use ur current location & get directions to somewhere. The map should

Cambria Hebert

pull up ur location when it pulls up directions. Text it to me.

Could this phone really be smart enough to know where I was? Was the signal strong enough for it to calculate a route while I was in a deep hole? How far off the beaten path did that man haul me? What if Nathan was too late? What if I was far away?

Enough. Just do it.

I snapped out of my internal freak-out and did as Nathan instructed. Why hadn't I thought of this? It made me angry that I hadn't. I knew I should give myself a break, that I was likely in shock, was injured and scared, but now wasn't the time for weak emotions. Now was the time for action.

It took the map a long time to load. The screen went dark twice while I waited. I stood and began pacing, unable to sit a second longer. My knees wobbled as I walked, but I ignored it and continued moving.

Finally, my location pulled up.

Reading a map wasn't one of my better abilities, so I took a screen shot and texted it to Nathan.

It failed the first time I tried to send it.

The second time took five minutes, but it went through. By the time the job was done, there was only thirty percent battery remaining.

I slid down into the dirt and leaned against the wall.

And I started to pray.

12

Nathan

I parked haphazardly in the yard by my house and rushed inside. I kicked off my sneakers and shoved my feet into my tan work boots. I tossed a ratty baseball cap on my head and went down into the unfinished basement and dug through my gear and loaded my pockets with everything I thought I might need.

My weapons were already in my Jeep.

Back upstairs, I shoved some vanilla-flavored power bars in my pockets and grabbed a bottle of water and a jacket on my way out the door. The sky was dark, no stars in sight, and the wind was picking up, making it feel much colder than it was outside.

I hoped Honor had some kind of protection from the elements wherever she was.

Once I was settled into the Jeep, the screenshot of the map came through my phone. I plugged my own phone into the car charger and turned on the engine. There in the darkness of the cab I studied the map.

It gave me a general idea where she was—about fifteen miles outside of the town of Slatington. She was definitely in the woods because there were no roads mapped around the little dot that marked her location.

I would drive as close as I could and then go on foot.

I decided to take the back roads, the ones least traveled. Due to the pileup, I figured a lot of the roads were going to be congested and I didn't want to get caught in it. I was glad when I got stationed here six months ago that I took the time to drive around, learn the area, and scout out roads.

It was more or less something I was trained to do and even though it wasn't really required for where I was working now, it was clearly proving useful.

As I drove, images assaulted me, images of the desert, of a gunfight, of blood. I shook my head, trying to clear my thoughts. The stress of the situation was just putting my mind into overdrive.

I felt this insistent need to find Honor, to save her. *Maybe it is because I wasn't able to save them.* The thought drew me up short, but once it was there, I couldn't deny it.

It was quite possible the reason I was going off alone, rogue, to find Honor was because I couldn't bear the thought of someone else dying—someone I knew I could help.

I turned off the main road and onto a lane that literally curved up the side of a mountain. The sign beside the gravel entrance read: **Travel at your own risk.**

I drove the Jeep forward. The sound of loose gravel hitting the underside of the vehicle was loud and startling in the dark. I continued up, looking at her map and cross-checking it with the one I had pulled up. The farther up I went, my headlights illuminated the narrow gravel road, and I hoped no one else was out driving tonight because only one car would fit at a time.

On the right side of the road was a steep drop. It was lined with trees and plants. I figured if something did happen and I happened to lose control and fall off, then I likely wouldn't plunge to my death. Surely the many trees would stop the Jeep from going too far.

Off to my right were more woods. I couldn't see very far in because it was so dark, but I figured if she was anywhere, it would be over to this side. When I realized I was around the area where she was, I stopped the Jeep and got out, walking into the trees to search for a place to put my Jeep. Leaving it out in the open seemed like a bad idea.

About a mile farther than I wanted to be was a small clearing beneath a canopy of trees. I jogged back to the car and drove it forward, using my four-wheel drive to go off the gravel road and basically four-wheel through the trees and over the uneven ground. I nudged the Jeep between two trees with low-hanging branches and then cut the lights and the engine.

I sat there a long time, listening to the sounds of the woods, wondering if anyone else was out there. The night remained still, except for the distant rumbling of thunder above.

I prayed the rain was moving away from us and not closer.

Before starting off on foot, I pulled out my phone and sent word to Honor. **I think I'm close by. If you hear me call out for you, answer.**

I didn't get a reply right away and I hadn't expected one. My service was low and I knew hers was worse. Hopefully she would at least get the message.

I palmed the pistol beneath the front seat and tucked it in the waistband of my jeans and then tucked the knife I always carried in my front pocket.

Then I pressed a few keys on my phone and held it to my ear.

Patton answered on the second ring. "Hallow," he drawled.

"Patton, this is Reed. Don't say my name."

"What's up?" he said, his tone staying the same, but I knew he was alert.

"You still playing poker?"

"Sure am!"

"Lex still there?"

He paused. I knew he wanted to ask me what this was about. I really hoped he didn't. "No."

I swore.

Patton stayed quiet on the other end of the line. Then I heard his muffled voice say, "I gotta piss."

I heard the opening and closing of two doors, and I imagined the path he was taking through the door by the bar, across the laundry room, and then into a tiny two-piece bathroom beside it.

"He left," Patton said, turning on the faucet as he talked.

"How long ago?"

"About thirty minutes." He paused. "He seemed a little distracted after you left."

Fuck. I probably shouldn't have pointed out his phone was missing. He hadn't known, and I called attention to it. I might have cost myself—and Honor—precious time. I was merely acting in the moment. I hadn't yet fully decided if those texts were the absolute truth. But once I saw his reaction to the missing phone, added to the picture and the necklace… I couldn't *not* believe it anymore.

"What's this about?" Patton asked, and I heard the sound of a toilet flush.

"I'll explain later," I said urgently. I needed to find her, and fast. "Don't tell anyone I called."

"I won't."

I pulled the phone away from my ear just as I heard Patton say, "Hey."

"Yeah?" I said.

"If you need anything, I got your back."

"Good to go," I replied.

"Semper Fi," Patton said and then he cut the line.

Semper Fi. Always faithful. It was the Marine Corps way of life. I knew if shit hit the fan, I could call and Patton would be there.

I hoped it didn't come to that.

I didn't bother to lock the Jeep when I got out and walked into the trees. I pulled the bill of my hat down low and tucked my hand in my jacket, pulling out a high-powered flashlight that was the size of a pen.

But in this case, size didn't matter.

This little baby would cut through the worst of the darkness tonight. Overhead, another rumble of thunder rolled. It covered the sound of a text coming through my phone.

I pulled it out, silenced the ringer, and looked down at the message.

Two words.

Two words that made my blood run cold.

He's back.

13

Honor

The thunder rolling through the night sky wasn't a good sign.

"Seriously," I muttered. "Like this day isn't bad enough?"

I guess when it rains it pours. Literally. I had very vivid imaginations of the sky opening up to some kind of freak torrential downpour and me being trapped in this hole as it slowly filled with icy cold rainwater. Slowly freezing or drowning me...

What would be a better way to go? Freezing to death or drowning?

I'm a writer and even I never dreamed up half this shit. Well, I guess one positive would be if I survived this, I would have a ton of new material to work with.

Thunder rumbled again, and I sighed. My stomach growled, matching the ferocity of the thunder, and I realized I hadn't eaten a thing all day. I never ate before my early runs because it upset my stomach. I usually made a pot of coffee and some kind of egg scramble after I returned home.

Then I would spend most of my day typing away at a story, social networking, marketing, and communicating with my agent.

I wondered if anyone noticed I was missing by now. I loved being a recluse, but I was beginning to think that my choice of lifestyle was a serious hazard.

Maybe I should have gotten a dog after all. A companion to have around all day might have been nice.

I paused. This was the second time today I thought of a dog. Why would I be thinking of something like that at a time like this?

I was insane. More so than usual. I was probably ready to suffer some sort of psychotic break from the stress of being kidnapped. I mean really, I thought I was stronger than that.

Or maybe you're just thinking of the things you never got to do.

I don't know where that inner voice was coming from, but it needed to shut up. I think I would prefer some psychotic break than sitting down here and thinking about the bucket list that was never fulfilled. I wasn't ready to admit defeat. I wasn't going to accept my death.

And also, I found it quite amusing that on the cusp of death, my one regret seemed to be that I didn't have a dog.

Of all the things I could regret, that was what I chose?

I had a feeling a psychiatrist would have a field day with that.

I looked up toward the top of the hole, and though it was dark, I could make out the tops of the trees swaying in the wind. I didn't want my kidnapper to come back, but I also didn't want to spend the entire night down here in the rain.

I pulled out the phone again and looked at the signal. No bars. I decided to distract myself by snooping. I called up the camera roll and started going through his pictures. They looked like pictures you'd find on any regular guy's phone. A barbeque, a baseball game, and one featuring the kidnapper front and center, with poker chips piled high in front of him.

Again, I was struck by how "normal" he appeared. How uncreepy and non-kidnapper-ish he seemed. He was the most dangerous kind of criminal of all because no one would suspect him. No one would be inclined to believe any accusations against him.

I flipped through a few more of the photos when one had me gripping the phone until the bones in my fingers ached.

It was of a young blond woman. She was smiling, but the smile didn't reach her eyes. Her eyes were haunted, they were sad… and they were also a little empty.

Around her neck was the locket I'd found in the dirt—the one now in my pocket.

My stomach roiled. Bile rose up in my throat and I dropped the phone and lurched to the side and heaved violently. Nothing came up because my stomach was empty. I made hideous sounds and the pain of retching had me collapsing onto the dirt floor and curling into a ball.

I lay there for a long time, feeling the cold dirt against my cheek and keeping my eyes closed, hoping I might wake up and find this was all dream.

Eventually, the uncomfortableness of my position made me roll over onto my back and stare up at the black sky.

Only there wasn't just black sky to look at.

There was something pale in my line of sight.

My heart rate accelerated when my eyes made out the shape of a man.

Nathan! He'd come for me after all!

"I told you I'd come back," intoned a voice from above.

Chills crawled up my spine and I shivered. That wasn't Nathan. It was my kidnapper.

"I had planned on leaving you down here for the night," he called. Funny how his voice didn't seem that far away; it seemed as though it was very close, and I reminded myself that he was up there and I was down here. For once, I didn't mind being down in this hole.

When I didn't respond to his comments, he spoke again.

"But it seems I have misplaced something. I came back to see if you had something of mine?"

My eyes darted to where the phone lay on the ground. It was facedown and the case was black. I knew he wouldn't be able to see it.

"Are you talking about your heart?" I snapped. "Cause I'm pretty sure you weren't even born with one."

"Feisty." He chuckled. "I like feisty. It turns me on."

Gag. Me. With. A. Spoon.

"It seems my cell phone has gone missing," he said. "You don't have it down there, do you?"

"If I did, I wouldn't still be here," I yelled.

"Well, that's good. Because I would hate to have to move up my timeline and just kill you now."

His timeline?

Something told me that being killed now versus later was probably the better option.

"I'm going to send down a rope ladder. Climb up," he said.

I wanted to laugh. *Yeah, right. And maybe monkeys will fly out of my ass.*

It was almost cute the way he tossed down the rope ladder and adjusted it so I could climb right up.

If pigs with mustaches and goatees were cute.

"Come on," he instructed.

"No."

The silence that followed my one-word reply was almost comical.

"What did you say?"

"I said I would rather sit down here and rot and die than climb up there and be any closer to you," I spat.

I heard his rough inhale and I knew I pissed him off.

Good. He pissed me off too.

"Get. Up. Here. Now."

"Why? So you can rape and murder me? No thanks. I'm not really feeling much like rape and murder today."

"You little bitch."

"I thought you said you liked my feisty attitude." I mocked. I knew I should shut up, but I found myself with a severe case of diarrhea of the mouth.

I sat down to punctuate my intention of doing exactly what he told me not to do. As I sat, I slowly pulled the phone into my palm and then crossed my hands over my chest, hiding it beneath my arm.

"How rude of me," he said in a conversational tone. "I realize my mistake."

Then he disappeared, leaving the rope hanging there, taunting me with freedom. I knew better. He probably wanted me to think he left so I would climb up to my doom.

While he was gone, I shoved the phone up my sleeve and then hooked my thumb through the little hole made into the arm. Hopefully that would be enough to keep the phone hidden.

A few minutes later, something hit me in the head.

I looked up only to see something else plummeting toward me, and I ducked just in time to avoid being hit in the face.

"What the hell?" I muttered and reached out to pick up the items he chucked down the hole at me.

My hand closed around one of the slightly textured, round items. It was an orange.

The crazy ass threw two oranges at me.

"I get grumpy when I don't eat, too," he said, like the reason I didn't feel like dying was because of low blood sugar.

There weren't enough M&Ms in the world for that. An orange sure as hell wasn't going to do it.

My stomach rumbled at the sight of it. I was tempted to peel it and dig in. But my writer's brain kicked in. He might have used a syringe and injected it with some sort of deadly poison.

I think I'd rather starve.

"Eat," he commanded.

I stood and threw the orange back up at him.

I was a girl. I threw like a girl.

The orange came back down and made a plopping sound at my feet.

"I would eat that if I were you," he growled.

I didn't bother to reply. I was exhausted, and fighting with him made it worse. I needed to save my strength for getting away.

I sat down in the dirt just as more thunder rolled overhead. I wished it would rain. I wished it would lightning and thunder and a storm of epic proportions would rage. It would chase him away. He would be forced to leave me here and not come back 'til morning.

Maybe by then, Nathan would have found me.

If he was even looking.

Let's face it here. My situation was pretty bleak. I was depending on a guy that I met through my kidnapper's phone. I highly doubted that he kept upstanding citizens as company. I more than likely texted his partner in crime. The pair of them had a good laugh at my expense and then creepy up there came back to throw oranges at my head and then murder me.

This wasn't one of my romance novels.

A dashing, romantic hero wasn't going to come riding up on his white horse and save me.

I was going to end up on the eleven o'clock news.

"Come on," the man above demanded.

"No!" I shouted.

"Fine!" he snapped. "If you won't come up, then I'll come down. It's a small space, but I'm sure we'll find room."

I shot to my feet. "I'm coming up."

He was already descending the ladder. I calculated my chances of yanking him off and beating him up before he overpowered me. Yes, he was bigger. Yes, he had weight on his side.

But I was seriously pissed.

(And I wanted to live to get a dog.)

"Fine, then. Hurry up. Or I'm coming down."

He went back up to ground level and stood, staring down. All I could see was the round paleness of his face against the dark backdrop of night. I walked over to the ladder and hunched over a little, acting as if I were defeated. Quickly, I pulled out the phone and shot off one last text to Nathan, taking a risk that maybe he was going to help me like he said.

"I'm waiting," he said angrily.

I tucked the phone back inside my sleeve and started to climb. I was freezing and surprisingly weak. It made climbing hard. I wasn't a large person, but I slipped a few times and my weight seemed like a lot to haul up a thirty-foot hole.

I took my time, trying to drag out the minutes while trying to formulate some sort of plan. The only plan I could come up with involved not dying.

I guess that meant as soon as my feet touched the ground, I needed to run like hell.

And hide. Hiding might be good.

He got impatient the closer I got and suddenly the rope ladder began to sway as he dragged it upward, bringing me with it. I started to slip and I gripped the rope tighter. The friction between the dirt wall and my fingers ripped open the skin on my knuckles. I bit my lip instead of crying out because I was still standing by my decision of not giving this guy one second of satisfaction.

When I got to the top, he gave the ladder one great yank and I spilled out over the lip, landing hard against my side and sharp pain radiating through my body. I was pretty sure at least a couple of my ribs were broken, and I was staring at the reason why.

Black boots (or shit kickers as some people might say) stepped into my line of vision, and anger swelled within me. It was those boots that nailed me in the ribs; it was those boots that snapped my bones.

I ignored the fierce burning of my scraped knuckles and pushed up onto my knees. He grabbed my hair and yanked me to my feet.

"This isn't the Stone Age," I griped. "You aren't a caveman. Quit pulling my hair."

Surprisingly, he let go of my ponytail.

Then he backhanded me across the face. I really, really hoped my other eye didn't swell shut. I kind of needed it to see.

"I've had enough of your attitude."

I'd had quite enough of his hitting, but I decided against saying so.

He moved to strike me again. My reflexes were faster. I threw my arm up to block the hit and then I kicked him in the shin.

I took off running, not knowing which direction to go, but not caring. Anywhere was better than here.

He tackled me (hadn't we played this out before?) and I fell, my face bouncing off the ground. The wind howled around us as my hand closed over a stick, and when he rolled me over, I swung it right at his head.

The tip of the makeshift weapon grazed his cheek and he grunted. Then he grabbed me around the wrist and yanked my arm away. He dug his fingers into my arm until I knew there would be bruises and he bent my wrist until the stick fell out of my grasp.

"What is this?" he asked, leaning down so even in the darkness I could see the wildness in his eyes. "What have you been hiding?"

His hand groped the shape of his phone beneath my sleeve.

I began to struggle, to kick and hit, to scream and shout. It wasn't enough to throw him off me, and he forced the phone—*his phone*—out of my sleeve.

He looked between me and the phone for long, seemingly endless seconds. The weight of his large frame pushed me into the ground, and my breath wheezed in and out of my lungs, every single inhale and exhale hurting.

Slowly, he reached out and unzipped my jacket.

My mind swam with ways I could kill him, with ways I could cause him pain.

"Get off me," I ground out.

He laughed.

His free hand pushed away the sides of my jacket, baring the white shirt I wore beneath. He made a tsking sound. "So many clothes you wear."

Then his hand closed over my breast. It was an effort to remain impassive as he roughly kneaded my skin.

He didn't even seem to notice he was fondling my breasts (thank God I was wearing a shirt and a sports bra) because he was too busy looking at his phone.

Please, Lord, don't let him look at the call history or the texts.

I knew the second he saw one or the other. His hand gripped my tender flesh and squeezed until I almost cried out. I knocked at his hand, dislodging the worst of his grip.

"You called 9-1-1?" he said, his voice low and flat.

Fear skittered along my nerve endings and the hair on the back of my neck stood tall.

"What did you tell them?" he said, looking at me over the phone.

I remained silent. My hand was lightly feeling around for a rock or another stick.

He gripped the front of my shirt and yanked me up so his face was inches from mine. "What did you tell them?"

"Nothing." I lied. "I couldn't get through. Your phone is a piece of shit."

He shoved me back onto the ground. My ears rang when my head recoiled off the ground. He was doing something on the phone again… I knew I needed to distract him.

Using all the energy I could muster, I twisted my entire body like I was rolling over. I knocked him over a bit and I jerked up, trying to get out from under him.

He leaned down, lying on top of me, using his entire body as a weight. His breath was hot against my ear. "I wouldn't do that if I were you," he began. "I'm already very angry."

I froze beneath him. Feeling his entire body against mine was disgusting. I was pinned down, completely at his will, and it made me sick.

He stoked my hair as he scrolled through the phone. Every once in a while, he would lick my ear. After a few minutes, his body went rigid.

I knew he found the texts.

Why hadn't I deleted them after I sent them?

His teeth closed over the sensitive flesh of my ear and he bit down. Hard.

I let loose a scream before I could stop myself. I felt my skin break and blood begin to ooze.

"Do you have any idea what you've done?" he shouted, rearing up.

He scrambled up and yanked me to my feet. I tried to run, but he pulled me back.

"You just sealed your fate," he spat. "What a pity too. I was so looking forward to getting to know that body of yours."

He hit me again, sending me flying backward onto the ground. I reached out for a stick, a rock, or something, but he leaped on me. He straddled my middle and then threw the phone behind my head. It hit a tree, and I heard it break.

The shattering of that phone took away any last hope of survival I had.

He reached behind him and pulled out something.

A very long, very sharp-looking knife.

"This is going to hurt," he promised.

My arms were pinned at my sides beneath his legs and my hands dug into the earth as he dragged the blade down the center of my chest.

I kicked up my legs, trying to bring them high enough to kick him in the back of the head. He laughed and pushed the blade against me harder.

I swallowed thickly and squeezed my eyes shut. Death was here.

14

Nathan

The sound of her scream had me spinning away from the direction I was heading and sent me running.

She was here. She was close. She screamed for a reason.

I prayed I wasn't too late and I moved stealthily over the uneven ground, dodging trees and branches as I ran. My heart rate wasn't erratic. My breathing was steady.

I was trained for this. I was trained to search through the woods, to find my way. I was trained to keep cool in bad situations. I was trained to run toward the danger and not away.

I heard Lex yell, his voice sounding more maniacal than I ever thought he was capable of, and I drew up, stopping my mad dash. I crept through the night, keeping my eyes peeled for a flash of movement, for the outline of a man.

Lightning cracked overhead, illuminating the sky, and it reflected off the wicked-looking blade of a knife.

In that split second, my brain processed the scene before me and sketched it out in my head as the sky went dark once more.

Lex had her pinned to the ground as she kicked her legs to no avail. He produced a knife, one that I had no doubt he had nefarious plans for. I thought about pulling out my pistol and taking a shot.

But the girl was wiggling too much; she was kicking too hard. What if I accidentally shot her? She was already wounded enough. I left my gun tucked in the waistband of my jeans and rushed forward. I had the element of surprise and the fact he was distracted immensely on my side.

I was on him before he realized his mistake. I grabbed him by the back of the neck and yanked him off her, tossing him onto the ground and then driving my fist into his jaw. It felt really good to punch this sick bastard in the face.

I got in another really good hit before Lex recovered and realized what was happening. With a great roar, he swiped at me with the knife. I pulled back in time to avoid the blade, and he leapt to his feet.

I heard movement behind me and I knew it was Honor, but I didn't turn to look at her. I kept my eyes trained on Lex and his knife.

"You should have stayed out of it," he spat.

"It's over. Just put the knife down."

In response, he lunged forward, swinging the blade. I spun away, but not before the edge caught on the sleeve of my jacket. The fabric made a sharp ripping sound.

I moved quickly, slamming my arm down across his elbow and making the knife drop to the ground. Then I kicked him in the kneecap and he stumbled.

Both of us pulled out a pistol at the same time. I trained mine on his chest. He trained his on Honor.

"Drop the gun," I demanded.

"I'll shoot her before you even pull the trigger," he said around a sick smile.

"Run," I told Honor.

When I didn't hear the scuffle of rushing feet, I yelled, "Run!"

I heard her then, retreating away from us.

Lex pulled the trigger. The sound of a bullet discharging from his weapon filled the air around us. Then he swung the gun at me and squeezed off a shot. I dove to the side and shot off a bullet of my own.

He went down at the same time I did. His bullet missed me, but I prayed to God mine hit him. He didn't move, and I hoped that meant he was injured.

I heard Honor yell my name, and I pushed off the ground and ran toward her yell. The chances of her being shot were high. If she was injured, I would need to get her out of here stat.

I saw the flash of her white shirt just ahead, and I dropped to my knees beside her.

"Are you hit?"

"Shot?" she asked, her breath coming in short spurts.

"Yes. Are you shot?"

"No."

"Good. Let's go."

I pulled her up and wrapped an arm around her waist. I started leading her away from Lex. We would have to take the long way around.

We made it about three steps.

Then she shocked the shit out of me by yanking the gun out of my hand and rushing away—back toward Lex.

"Honor!" I yelled, thinking this chick must be out of her mind.

I ran behind her and she tore through the woods, skidding to a stop beside the manmade hole that was dug into the ground.

"Where is he!" she demanded, holding the gun out in front of her like she meant business.

My eyes went to the spot where he fell.

It was empty.

"Come on you sick bastard!" she challenged. "Not so tough when the playing field is even!"

She stole my gun and ran back to where she was being held captive with the intention of shooting her captor?

She was one crazy bitch.

It was awesome.

Nothing around us moved and as awesome as her kickass attitude was, it was also kind of stupid. He had a gun. He could be lining up a shot right that minute.

My gut told me he ran off, but I wasn't going to take any chances.

I approached Honor like a cowboy approaching a nervous filly. "Hey," I said gently. "It's okay now. He ran off."

She still stood rigidly, holding the gun out in front of her like she would shoot anything that freaking dared to breathe.

"Honor," I said, stopping at her side. "You're safe now." Slowly, I reached out and wrapped my hand over the gun, pulling her arm down and gently taking the pistol from her grasp.

I wrapped my hand around the back of her neck. Her skin was ice cold to the touch. The warmth of my palm seemed to break through whatever mental state she was in and she turned her head, her eyes searching for mine in the dark.

"You came," she whispered like she never really thought I would.

Something inside me cracked at her tiny, whispered words. "Of course I came."

She folded herself against my chest, pressing her face into my jacket and letting out a deep exhale. My arm left her neck and wound around her, clutching her against me, supporting her weight, and noting how small she felt in my arms.

She might be tiny, but she was a survivor.

"You did good, sweetheart," I murmured. "You did real good."

I felt a shudder move through her and I wanted to gather her even closer. I was tempted to sit down right there on the ground and pull her into my lap and hunch myself around her, to shelter her with my body.

But I couldn't.

We had to get out of here.

Lex might not be in sight, but that didn't mean he wasn't lurking.

"We gotta get out of here," I told her. "Can you walk?"

She stayed curled against me for a minute longer and then she looked up. Even in the darkness, I could see the swelled area of her eye, make out the bruises all over her face.

Cold fury rose up within me and seeped right into my bones. Men who hit women were the lowest of low. There was a special place in hell for SOBs like Lex.

"I can walk," she said, reminding me that I asked a question.

"Come on," I said, tucking my arm around her waist. She stiffened and I moved to pull back, but her hand caught mine and pulled it back around her.

She looked up, giving me a sheepish look. "You're warm."

My lip lifted in half a smile and then I stopped. I was an ass. I pulled my arms free and quickly pulled off my jacket. "Here," I said, wrapping it around her.

She sighed like she was in heaven and pushed her arms through. I tried not to be endeared by the fact that the sleeves hung well past her hands, but a guy could only withstand so much.

I reached between us and fumbled with the zipper, finally getting it to catch and then sliding it up right beneath her chin. The black fleece swallowed her whole.

It was cute as hell.

"Come on," I said gruffly, not really knowing how a woman I just met could climb under my skin so fast.

I told myself it was her bravery, her willingness to fight for her life.

But really, I think it had more to do with how she felt fitted against my side.

"Do you think he'll come back?" The fear in her voice made her sound vulnerable.

"If he does, I'll kill him." The words weren't meant to make her feel better. Those words were the truth. The next time I saw Lex, I was going to kill him.

It took forever to get back to the Jeep. Honor's movements began to slow the farther we walked. She held herself stiffly, and I knew she was injured in places I couldn't see.

This sick, twisty feeling took over my gut as ideas of what he did to her stole my thoughts. I wanted to ask, but I was afraid I would upset her.

"That's my Jeep up ahead," I told her when I saw its dark shape come into view.

"Thank God," she murmured, stumbling a little.

My grip tightened around her waist, trying to keep her from falling. She yelped. I jerked back like I'd been burned.

"What?" I hadn't been rough.

"Sorry," she replied, hunching over a bit. "I think my ribs are broken."

Shit, I'd been holding her around the middle the entire trek back to the Jeep. It had to have been killing her. "Why didn't you say something?" I said harshly.

Her head swung in my direction. "Because it doesn't change anything. We have to get out of here."

She was right. I hated it.

I took her hand, knowing not to touch her middle, but not being able to *not* touch her at all. I led her to the Jeep where it sat partially concealed by the trees.

Something was wrong…

I squinted at the dark shape of the vehicle again, trying to figure out what wasn't right. I pulled the flashlight out of my pocket and aimed it at my car.

It was sitting lopsided.

I directed the beam at the tires.

They were slashed.

We weren't going to be driving anywhere.

15

Honor

As I was staring at the slashed and unusable tires, the sky chose that moment to open and throw down some rain.

Yay.

Nathan's jacket had warmed me up. The fat icy drops now lunging from the sky were likely going to hinder that a bit.

"Get in," Nathan said over the roar of the rain, pulling open the driver's side door and ushering me into the tiny back seat of the Wrangler.

After I was in, he got in the driver's seat and shut the door behind him. I collapsed against the seat, thinking that being in this cramped Jeep was the most comfortable place I'd ever been. Never mind the seats were vinyl and not all that warm. Never mind the tires were ruined and we couldn't actually drive anywhere.

In that moment, I was just thrilled to be out of that hole, away from that vile man, and out of the rain.

Everything else was just details.

Right?

Okay, no.

"I don't suppose you have several spares in the back and not just one?" I asked.

He grunted. "No."

"Well, shit."

"Yep."

"Where do you think he is?" I whispered, the words refusing to come out any louder.

He turned in his seat and looked at me through the dark. I wished it was light enough for me to make out his features. I really wanted to *see* him. So far, all I could make out was that he was tall and broad with short, dark hair.

"He's still out there," he said, grim. I shot at him, but the bullet might have just nicked him because I was moving when I fired. "He's obviously still pissed too."

"Because of the tires, you mean?" I guess it was a dumb question. People who weren't angry didn't go around slashing other people's tires.

"Yeah. And because you got away." He was silent a moment. "Guys like him don't like to lose. They like to be in control."

I shuddered a little at his words. My kidnapper was definitely big on control. "I called 9-1-1. I told her my name, but the phone was disconnected."

"I went to the police too. There was some bad accident out on Route 210. A lot of casualties. The police station was practically empty when I got there."

"That's why you came," I whispered.

"You needed someone fast."

Yeah, I did. And he came. Emotion swelled up in my chest, choking me up. I swallowed it down. "Thank you," was all I could manage. Why is it those words never seem like enough?

"You're welcome." The reply was a soft whisper that floated to me from the front of the cab. His words were simple too. They were more than enough.

He opened up the center console of the Jeep and pulled out some sort of energy bar. "Here," he said, handing it back to me.

I took his offering, ripped open the wrapper, and bit into the sweet food. I made a sound of appreciation when vanilla burst over my tongue.

"How long were you down there?" he asked, his voice strained.

"He took me this morning. I was out for a run on the trail."

"So like fifteen hours," he surmised.

"I guess," I replied around a large bite of food. It had felt like forever.

As soon as the bar was finished, I crumpled the wrapper and stuck it the jacket pocket. A bottle of water appeared in my line of vision.

I took a small sip at first, the cool water slipping down my parched throat with ease.

"What did he do to you?" Nathan whispered. His voice was hoarse.

I paused my drinking and lowered the bottle against my chest. "It could have been worse."

"You're bleeding."

I glanced down at my hand holding the bottle. I'd forgotten about the raw state of my knuckles. "I'll be okay."

He didn't say anything but went back to rummaging through the center console. When he closed the lid, he held up a small white kit. "I'm coming back there."

Before I could protest that there was no way we would both fit, he squeezed himself between the seats and mushed his wide frame beside me.

He smelled good. Like a fresh-cut Christmas tree.

He held up the tiny flashlight, which was surprisingly strong, and handed it to me. "Here, point this at your hands. Keep the light trained down."

"What if he sees?" I worried, glancing out the very dark window. I could see nothing. The sound of the rain pounding against the ragtop was very loud, and the wind rocked the vehicle occasionally.

"If he comes here, I'll shoot him." There was no room for doubt in his words. In fact, his voice held a backbone of steel that made me a little nervous.

"It's not that bad." I tried. "I can wait." Okay, so since he reminded me of my injuries, they hurt like hell. But I wasn't going to admit that.

"Honor," he said gently, all traces of the steel gone. He didn't just say my name—he breathed it. It was like he inhaled it into his body, filled up his lungs, and then exhaled.

Something warm spread throughout me, like I was being warmed up from the inside out.

"There's no reason to leave it like that when I can clean it up."

He didn't touch me. Maybe he knew I was still kind of in shock from everything that happened.

I was.

But damn, I wanted him to touch me.

He placed the small kit on his lap and popped it open, reminding me of an oversized kid with his lunchbox. "This is probably going to hurt like a bitch."

I laughed. Thank God he wasn't the kind of guy to say, "This might hurt a little," when we all knew that it was going to hurt way more than that.

He was looking at me when I placed my hand between us. "What?" I said, my heart lodging in my throat and making it very hard to breathe.

"You have a good laugh."

I didn't say anything because my throat was still obstructed and now my stomach was doing all kinds of funny flips. I really hoped the bar I just inhaled didn't make a reappearance. I turned on the light and shined it down low between us over the bloody mess that was my hand.

He used his teeth to rip open some kind of little wipe. "Ready?" he murmured, slipping a free hand beneath mine.

I nodded.

He was right. The process of cleaning my scraped and raw knuckles hurt. It hurt a lot. But the good thing was I barely registered the pain because I was too entranced by the feeling of his skin against mine.

Too entranced by sitting there in a tiny enclosed space with a very large man while he protectively curled his body close to mine and cupped my hand with his. The sound of falling rain splattering against the ragtop and sliding down the vinyl windows was so melodic that if I wasn't in survival mode, I might have been lured to sleep.

The scent of pine wrapped around me, bringing me comfort as I stared at the top of his dark head bowed laboriously over my hand. If he noticed the way the flashlight shook in my hand, he didn't comment.

Nothing had ever affected me this way. Not ever.

I tried to commit this feeling to memory, the exact sound of his breathing, the way our knees bumped together. It sort of felt like we were in a small cocoon, closed off from the world. Safe.

Feeling safe had become a real luxury.

I tried to tuck away every detail for later when I was able to sit down at the keyboard and write. Yes, I guess I was thinking about work. But when you do what you love, it isn't work. And when every experience, every single aspect of life can be pulled on for inspiration... well, even my own kidnapping is fair game.

And so was Nathan.

He was far more interesting than any story I could ever write about myself.

"Almost done," he spoke, bringing me out of my head and back in the moment with him.

I watched him gently spread some antibacterial cream over the worst of the scrapes and then individually wrap each of my four fingers in separate Band-Aids.

"That looks ridiculous." I scoffed. "They probably won't stay on."

"They'll stay," he stated, smoothing the last one into place.

"How do you know?" Little tingles shot up my arm and into my elbow. It made me feel all squirmy inside.

He looked up, our eyes connecting in the dim light created by the flashlight. "Because I put it there."

I would have called him on his arrogance… if I could've found the oxygen to speak.

The temperature in the Jeep rose about twenty degrees as we stared at each other silently. It was like there was some sort of pull between us, a special gravity that only he and I could feel. The air between us practically crackled with tension—but not the stressful kind, the good kind. The kind of tension that made me bite the inside of my lip and squeeze my thighs together.

After several charged moments, he broke eye contact. I was partially relieved, partially disappointed. Nathan ripped open yet another of those wipe thingies. The flash of his straight white teeth as he used them had me biting the inside of my lip even harder.

He shook out the mini towelette and looked up. Without warning, without a single word, he cupped the back of my head, his palm completely spanning the base of my skull. His warmth seeped into my scalp and sent little goose bumps racing over me. They multiplied so fast it almost felt like a million tiny ants rushed over my body.

I couldn't hold back the shiver.

"You cold?" he asked.

"Not as cold as before."

His fingers flexed into my hair and he reached up, using the wipe to gently dab at my lower lip. "What happened here?" he asked gently.

I swallowed. "I'm not sure." It could have been from me biting it. It could have been from being hit. Who knew?

He grunted and pulled it away, and I caught a glimpse of the dark stain against the white. He folded it over and then returned, swiping carefully over more of my skin. "I'm not going to be able to do anything about that eye right now."

"It's okay."

"It's not," he said, that steel creeping back into his tone. His shoulders stiffened slightly and I tensed. In that moment, he seemed like a cornered, aggressive animal. Like he was seconds away from completely losing it.

He took a deep breath and expelled it, the action seeming to calm him down. "It makes me angry he did this to you."

"Are you friends with him?" I couldn't keep the question in any longer.

He tossed the wipe into his lap with the other used one. "No," he replied.

"Then how come you texted him?"

"I play poker once a week with a group of guys. Lex is one of them. He was late to the game and I texted to see if he was coming."

"His name is Lex?"

Nathan nodded.

Putting a name to the hideous man who tortured me didn't make him seem any more human. In fact, it made him seem like more of a monster.

"I had no idea he was a total whack job."

"Well, he is that," I agreed.

Nathan flashed a grin in the darkness. I longed to see him in the light. I wanted to know the angles and planes of his face. I wanted to take in his features and truly see the man who had literally saved my life.

Nathan seemed oblivious to my thoughts as I watched him tidy up the first aid kit. Before he put it on the floor, he glanced at me. "Where else are you hurt?"

"I won't be requiring any more Band-Aids," I quipped.

He turned to look at me fully. His hand closed over mine and he gently took the flashlight from my grasp and clicked it off. "What about your ribs?"

"I don't think you have anything in that kit for them."

"Let me see them."

"Wh-what?" My mouth ran dry. He wanted to look under my shirt?

"I want to see them."

"That's not really necessary—"

He studied me and then thrust his hand out in the space between us. "Hey, I'm Nathan Reed. It's nice to meet you."

I wanted to laugh. We were a little beyond a formal introduction. But it was fun (hey, you try being kidnapped and beaten and see what you consider fun), so I slid my hand into his. "I'm Honor."

He held my hand a little longer than he needed to, his thumb brushing over the inside of my wrist. I caught myself right before I started purring like a cat.

That would have been hella embarrassing.

"I'm a staff sergeant in the United States Marine Corps. My favorite color is green, and I like football."

"What are you doing?" I asked, thoroughly charmed by him.

"Formally introducing myself so you'll let me under your shirt."

I laughed. "I usually don't let men I just met under my shirt."

"I'm irresistible."

I smiled. "And so modest."

"Now you know all about me. Your turn."

I lifted my eyebrow. I knew all about him? I highly doubted that. In fact, Nathan Reed seemed like a guy with many layers. But I played along.

"I'm Honor Calhoun. I'm a writer. My favorite color is blue, and I also like football."

"You like hot wings, Honor?" he asked like it was the most important thing he needed to know.

"Who doesn't?"

"Nice," he drawled. He had quite the southern accent going. Every time he talked, I felt a little giddy and I hung on every word he said. I was waiting for him to drop his first "y'all."

"All right," he said, gesturing to my shirt. "Lift it up. Let's see it."

"You suck at foreplay."

He caught my wrist in his oversized palm and towed me a little closer. His face came close to mine, so close that I was able to see that he had blue eyes and a scar across one of his cheeks. "That, sweetheart, was not foreplay. When we get to that, you'll damn well know it."

Well, alrighty then.

Shamelessly, I wondered when we might get to the foreplay.

He released my wrist and tugged at the hem of my shirt and jacket. He wasn't going to relent, that much was clear. I sighed and slapped away his hand.

Then I opened up the jacket. Before I could get the zipper down, he was sliding up my jacket and shirt, bunching it up beneath my breasts, and then the tiny light clicked back on.

When the beam met with my torso, breath hissed out between his teeth. "What the fuck did he do to you?"

I glanced down long enough to see purple and black splotches all over my creamy skin. The area was puffy and grotesque looking, and I turned away. I didn't want to see it. Feeling it was bad enough.

"He kicked me."

A low growl ripped from his throat.

I glanced at him, expecting to see rage taking over his face, but instead he wore a frown. Ever so lightly, he brushed the tips of his fingers over the area and I winced. Even his soft caress hurt.

And then he did something I didn't see coming.

The flashlight fell from his fingertips and rolled into the crack of the seat, plunging the backseat back into darkness. Nathan's newly free hand wrapped around my lower back, his palm spanning my waist as he ducked his head and pressed his lips to the injured area.

He trailed barely there kisses across the extremely tender flesh.

Who the hell needed a Band-Aid when he was around?

"I'm sorry," he whispered, looking up. "I'm not the one who did this and I can't take away the pain, but if I could…"

He didn't finish the sentence, but the unspoken dangled there between us and made me forget every ache that coursed through my body.

In that moment, I fell just a little bit in love with him.

16

Nathan

Her injuries pissed me off.

And what pissed me off more was the fact that she didn't whine or complain about them. No, I didn't want to hear some whiny female sniveling all over the place, but fuck. She earned it. I can't even imagine the crap she'd been through in the last fifteen hours.

She was going to end up like me.

Messed up.

She deserved better than that.

I didn't know her, but I knew enough to realize that kind of life wasn't what I wanted for her. Hell, I wouldn't wish this shit on my worst enemy.

Okay. Maybe I would.

But not her.

Never Honor.

God. Just her name in my thoughts was enough to stir up things in me that had laid dormant to the point I thought they went extinct. It was a freaking dandy time for them to show up out of the blue.

Especially in this situation.

Especially given what I had to do.

I fished the flashlight out of the crack between the seat and straightened. "We need to go."

"Go?" she said. Her eyes widened and looked like two large white marbles.

"We can't stay here. We're sitting ducks."

"It's raining."

Yeah, it was. "Exactly."

"You need to explain," Honor said, pushing herself up a little higher in the seat. She tried to hide the grimace of pain that crossed her face. I saw it. It pissed me off further.

"Lex slashed my tires. He wants us stranded. He wants us vulnerable. He's out there. He's going to be looking for us. He doesn't want us to get out of these woods alive."

"He's going to kill us?" The veiled fear in her words caused my gut to tighten.

"We're not safe yet. You might be out of that hole, but he still wants us dead. Now more than ever. If we get out of here, there's going to be a manhunt for that bastard, and I'll lead the team."

"I already called the cops."

"That's good. I'll call them too, have them send someone out here." I probably should have called them when I got here, but I hadn't wanted to call if she wasn't here. I wanted to find her first. Of course, once I found her, I was too busy to call anyone.

"We know who he is. What he's done." Honor seemed to be reasoning it out for herself so I didn't bother to reply. I watched as she reached under my jacket and pulled out the necklace I saw in the photo. "He's done this before," she said, her voice wavering. "We have to stop him."

"We will. It's why we can't stay here. He will be expecting us to take refuge from the rain. He'll expect you to be too weak to go on foot."

"I'm not weak."

I smiled a little. She was like a kitten with a really big roar. "I know you aren't."

"So what's the plan?"

"The plan is to get moving, work our way to the road."

"It's dark. How will we know which direction to go?"

I was insulted. "Sweetheart," I drawled. "I was trained for this. I could find my way out of a pig's ass."

"How the hell would you get into a pig's ass?"

"Exactly."

She snorted. It wasn't very ladylike. It was cute as hell. "You make no sense."

"You're going to make me into one of the characters in your next book, aren't you?" I couldn't help but tease her.

"Yes. He's going to have no teeth and one eye."

I chuckled. "Wow, you got good eyesight. I was hoping the dark would disguise my ugly ass 'til morning."

"Whatever," she tossed out.

As much as I wanted to sit here all night in this godforsaken tiny-ass back seat, I knew we had to go. We'd been here too long as it was. Before, I just didn't have the heart to make her run off in the rain. She'd been standing there with this lost, hopeless look written all over her, and I could see the dark smudges of dried blood on her skin.

I knew I needed to assess her injuries and she needed a moment to rest.

But rest was over.

We had to move.

I picked up the water bottle she abandoned and handed it to her. "Drink some of this."

As she drank, I pushed up out of the seat and climbed back up front. "I know you're looking at my ass," I told her as I moved.

I heard the sound of water spraying out of her mouth. "It's too dark too see anything in here."

"Didn't keep you from looking anyway," I quipped as I slid into the driver's seat and opened the center console. I grabbed the rest of the power bars and the second bottle of water. "Put these in your pocket," I said, handing her the bars.

Then I stretched over into the passenger side and felt around under the seat until my hand closed over the extra pistol I kept there.

"You know how to shoot a gun?"

"Nope."

I passed it back to her. "Safety's off. Point it and then pull the trigger."

"What if I shoot myself?"

"Don't."

"Thanks for the lesson."

"Anytime, babe."

Her muffled giggle made me smile.

"You ready?"

All traces of the joking, friendly air that surrounded us up until that point now vanished.

"Yeah."

Just as I was about to open the door, the sound of a blasting gun cut through the rain. Honor screamed as a bullet tore through the back of the ragtop.

"Get down!" I roared, flinging open the door and rolling out of the Jeep and across the ground. From my roll, I moved right into a low crouch, with the pistol cocked and ready in my hand. My eyes scanned the darkness and my ears trained on every single sound I heard.

I duck-walked toward the Jeep, keeping my back to the vehicle and my eyes open. Another bullet cut through the night, and I turned my head in the direction of the sound. Then I edged my way to the back side of the Jeep and fired off three rapid shots in the direction the bullets came from.

"Let's go!" I whispered to Honor, leaning in the back seat and reaching down to the floorboard to practically yank her onto the ground.

She stumbled a bit but recovered quickly.

"If anyone, and I mean anyone, comes near us, freaking shoot them."

She nodded sagely and I backed us up so we moved around the front of the car. All of a sudden, a bunch of thrashing in the woods behind us caused my heart to leap.

I fired off another shot and then dragged Honor off to the side and crouched behind some overgrown trees and shrubs.

The rain was still falling in heavy sheets, my clothes were soaked through already, and the wind made it feel a lot colder than it really was.

I placed a finger over my lips and looked at Honor. She rolled her eyes as if to say, "Well, duh."

She mouthed the word "run" to me, and I shook my head.

Running wasn't my style.

Outsmarting idiots was.

We sat there for a while. The waiting game was long and arduous, but I knew eventually I would win.

It was probably an hour when I caught the first sign of movement near the Jeep.

Lex was creeping up to the back. I raised my gun to take a shot, but he quickly moved, rushing to the opposite side of the Jeep, hiding him from view.

I watched as he walked slowly, his head appearing over the hood. "Come out, come out, wherever you are," he called.

Did he really think we would listen? Idiot.

I realized then that he was enjoying this. It was like a sport to him. It was likely the reason he dumped Honor in a hole and left her there. He liked the anticipation. Knowing she was down there, knowing he could have her whenever he wanted.

And now he anticipated a hunt.

I watched him move. One side of his body was a little lower than the other. He seemed to favor the right side over the left.

I knew then I'd managed to shoot him. It couldn't have been that bad of a wound if he was still up and walking around.

But at least he was injured. He would get tired faster. He wouldn't move as quickly as us.

He stopped at the hood of the Jeep and stared off into the woods just ahead. He seemed to listen for some kind of sound, but the heavy rain drowned out whatever he hoped to hear. Finally, he began walking again. I thought about taking the shot, about trying to drop him right there.

But what if I missed?

What if he managed one last shot after I hit him? What if that shot hit Honor??

Any mistakes I made could cost Honor her life. I couldn't live with another death on my conscience. Maybe it wasn't very Marine-like, but our best bet was to run, to get away. Outsmarting him was one thing, but engaging in enemy fire with some desperate crazy man wasn't a good idea.

When Lex disappeared from sight, heading the way he thought we went, I made my move. I took Honor's hand and stealthily led her in the direction from which Lex had just come. I didn't think he would double back the way he just came.

Of course, I wasn't one hundred percent sure… but it was a chance I was willing to take.

17

Honor

Nathan walked behind me. I knew it was because he intended to block any bullets that might fly our way.

I thought he was crazy when he suggested we leave the protection of the Jeep and set off on foot, but once the shooting started, I realized maybe he was right. He said he was a Marine. That was a good thing, right? I mean, any time anything bad happened in the news or a new war broke out; it was the Marines that were called in.

I found myself wondering what he looked like in uniform.

Yes, they were inappropriate thoughts for a time like this. But my brain needed a break from all the killing and the people wanting me dead stuff. Imagining Nathan in a uniform was a good distraction.

The rain still hadn't let up. My Nikes were soaked through and caked with mud. My pants were drenched and my hair was plastered to my head in what I knew was probably most unflattering.

At least it was dark.

Every step I took caused pain to radiate through my middle, and the scrapes on my face burned when the rainwater dripped into them (which was pretty much every single second). We didn't talk; we just walked. Nathan set a pace that was at times punishing. I didn't complain because I knew he was just trying to get us out of there.

Hell, the faster we got out of these godforsaken woods, the faster we would be safe.

I wondered about Lex and where he was. Every odd sound I heard, every snapping of a branch, would send me into a panic as my body readied to leap out of the path of a barreling bullet.

My foot plopped down in a slick puddle of mud and my arms shot out from my sides, trying to balance, trying to prevent me from falling. But then my other foot started to slide around and I knew I was going down.

Just before I landed in a heap of mud, Nathan caught me around the waist and pulled me close.

"Careful," he whispered, helping me back onto my feet. He held onto my arm as I stepped out of the mud and onto sturdier land. "Come on," he said, leading me off to the side, beneath a very large tree.

The branches overhead still contained enough leaves to shelter us from the worst of the rain. I don't know if it was my imagination, but it seemed warmer under here.

Or maybe it was because Nathan was inches away from me and his body heat was sinful.

He leaned up against the rough bark of the tree, planting his feet wide. I was close enough to see the outline of his hard chest and torso through the wet shirt that was plastered against his frame.

Clearly, he worked out. A lot.

"Come here," he said quietly, holding out one of his arms and inviting me close.

I hesitated a fraction of a second and then stepped between his legs as he pulled me in so I was leaning right up against him. Even though he was soaking wet, he still radiated heat. My icy cold fingers curled closer to him from within the sleeves of his fleece jacket.

"Why don't you rest for a minute?" he suggested right into my ear. "We've been walking a long time."

My legs were shaking. From the effort of walking? From the fear of being hunted? From being so close to him? I didn't know. But no matter how stiffly I held myself, they refused to stop.

Nathan slid down the trunk of the tree until his butt hit the pile of fall-colored leaves. He tugged me into his lap and used his hand to tuck my cheek against his chest.

It was an awfully intimate position. But he was so warm and his presence was so reassuring. I didn't want to move. So I stayed.

He used his fingers to pull the wet strands of my dark hair off my face and tuck them behind my ear. The steady rhythm of his heartbeat caused my eyes to droop closed. I was so incredibly tired. My body felt like a bowl of Jell-O, all wobbly and loose.

"Do you think he's following us?" I whispered.

"Maybe."

"How much longer until we hit the road?"

"We should have hit it a while ago, but I had to double back because I thought I heard him heading in our direction."

I glanced up. "Why didn't you say anything?"

I felt him shrug as he pushed my head back against his chest. "It wouldn't have changed anything," he replied, running his fingers through my wet hair. "Besides, you're scared enough."

"I'm not scared enough for you to keep the truth from me," I snapped.

His fingers paused. "I wasn't trying to lie."

I sighed. "I know. I'm sorry."

His fingers began stroking me again. My eyes slid closed. "We have maybe a mile or two before we hit a road. We will follow it until we find someone."

"Should we call the police?"

"I'll call them when we hit the road. I'm not sure how near he is, and I don't want to make too much noise. Plus, it will be easier for them to find us."

Every once in a while, a big fat rain drop would drip off the leaves above and hit me on the cheek. It would trail over my skin like I was crying, even though I wasn't.

"I'm going to get a puppy," I announced, not really sure why I was bringing this up again.

"Oh yeah?" he asked. His voice vibrated in his chest and tickled me.

I nodded against him. "Yeah. I've always wanted a dog."

"What kind of dog do you want?"

"I have no idea." I giggled. "I didn't know I wanted one so bad until today."

"Staring down death has a way of making things clear."

"You say that like you understand."

He didn't reply.

"How long have you been a Marine?"

"Six years."

"How old are you?" I asked.

"Twenty-four. I joined the Corps right out of high school."

"I didn't know there were Marines in this area."

"I'm stationed in Allentown. It's a very small reservist base."

"You live out in this area?" I asked, curious.

"Mmmm," he replied. "I like to get away at the end of the day."

"Are you from the South?"

"You like my accent?" he asked, a smile in his voice.

"Maybe," I said, smiling.

He chuckled. "Born and raised in North Carolina."

"This your first time being stationed up North?"

"Yep."

Without realizing it, I cuddled in a little closer and he tightened his hold on my body. I felt his chin rub the top of my head, and I took a deep breath. "You smell like a Christmas tree."

"Is that a good thing or a bad thing?"

"My favorite holiday is Christmas," I said shyly.

He started stroking my hair again.

"Not many people would have come looking for me," I told him, wondering what he would say. Because of me, he'd been shot at, punched, stranded in the woods, and now forced to hike through the rain with an injured woman.

"The police were busy."

"You could have left them all the information and gone home."

"I don't leave behind people in trouble."

Again, I sensed more behind his words than he said, but I didn't feel like it was my place to ask. "Well, whatever your reason… thank you."

"You already thanked me."

"Words are never enough."

"Aren't you a writer?" he asked, amusement in his tone.

I laughed. It hurt my ribs. "Yeah."

"Bake me a pie."

"What?" I asked, wondering how the topic turned to food.

"You can thank me by baking a pie."

"You like pie?"

"Who doesn't?"

He had a point. He was probably one of those bachelors who never cooked… Wait a minute… *bachelor.* "Are you married?"

"No."

"Girlfriend?"

"No."

"I find that hard to believe."

"You haven't really seen my face yet," he replied, amused.

I didn't need to see his face. I knew he was beautiful.

"What kind of pie do you want?" I said, getting back on topic.

"Apple."

"Apple pie it is." Nearby, a branch snapped. Nathan's entire body changed. He went from relaxed and playful to tensely gripping the gun. He moved swiftly, placing me between the trunk of the tree and his body as he scanned the area around us.

When no gunshots rang out and Lex didn't appear, he reached around and took my hand. "We need to keep moving."

As we walked, he felt in his back pocket and pulled out his cell phone. The cell phone that started it all, the cell phone that kept me alive.

He pressed the button at the bottom, but nothing happened. He did it again and again. Nothing. He stopped walking and we both stared down at the inoperative phone.

"Shit," he swore. "It got too wet."

"How much longer?" I worried.

He looked through the dark. Off in the distance was an obscure, hulking shape. Fear made my belly bottom out.

"Thank fucking God," he said and took my hand, dragging me along behind him. His legs were much longer than mine, and I had to practically run to keep up.

"What is that?" I asked between gasping for breath. I kind of assumed it wasn't something bad like I supposed before, judging from the way he used breakneck speed to get there.

I stared through the pounding rain again and realized what it was he was so anxious to get to.

A car.

A truck to be exact.

A black pickup truck sitting right there in the open.

For some reason, a memory of banging around in the bed of that truck washed over me. I tripped and stumbled. Nathan tried to haul me up, but I fell anyway, landing on my knees on the soaking ground.

"Honor?"

"It's Lex's," I whispered, feeling sick. I barely remembered anything about the trip here.

Until I saw that truck.

Memories washed over me and I started to retch. The protein bar I'd eaten hours ago came up with violent force.

A string of cuss words came from above me, but I barely heard them. I was too busy barfing. Tears leaked down my face. I wasn't crying, but the force of my heaving pushed them out of my eyes.

Nathan dropped to his knees beside me. It was like he didn't care about what I was doing at all. His warm hands gathered the loose, wet strands of my hair and pulled them back while he murmured words that were meant to comfort me.

Finally, thankfully, I stopped.

I would have collapsed in the mess I just made, but he caught me and hauled me into his lap. I really liked sitting in his lap.

I hated being so vulnerable. Yet my body couldn't take anymore. I was a strong person, but everyone had their limits.

He rocked me back and forth, holding me close while the rain fell in sheets around us. He didn't tell me I was being a baby. He didn't tell me we had to go. He acted as if we had all the time in the world and he would hold me as long as I wanted.

I couldn't even properly appreciate that because I was being assaulted.

Assaulted by images I had no doubt my mind had pushed away to protect itself.

I hit the bottom of the truck bed. The rough Rhino liner scraped my knee. He had tied my hands behind my back and then rolled me so I was lying on top of them.

He stood above me, staring down… hatred and lust glittering in his cold eyes.

I didn't know lust and hatred could ever go together.

But there was no denying the lust.

Because he unzipped his jeans and pulled out his very hard penis. I gagged at the sight. Fear of what he planned to do overwhelmed me.

I struggled. I tried to pull my hands free. I tried to protect myself.

He dropped to his knees, straddling my chest. He shoved himself in my face, demanding I take him in my mouth.

His satiny skin pushed at my lips, trying to get me to open up, trying to get me to let him in.

I opened up all right. And I screamed my head off.

My captor looked around sharply, like he was afraid someone would hear. Then he trained his angry gaze back down at me, took a handful of my hair, and slammed my head into the floor.

I blinked, trying to recall what happened next, but I couldn't. I must have blacked out from the hit. Automatically, my hand reached up to the back of my neck and delved into my hair. There in the center of my head was a bump.

I thought my headache was because I was hungry and weak.

But now I knew differently.

"What's going on, Honor?" Nathan said, his voice a little desperate.

"I remembered something," I said hollow. "Something I'd… forgotten."

He made a sound in the back of his throat. In one swift move, he stood, bringing me with him. He cradled me against his chest like a child. I tried to tell him I would walk, but when I glanced back at the truck, the words died on my lips.

"Are we taking that?" I asked shakily.

"Yep."

I began to shake. He stopped and looked between me and the truck. His lips turned into a thin, straight line.

"I'll be okay," I said, forcing my voice to be strong. That truck was our way out of this hell. I wasn't about to make things harder than they were.

He nodded briskly and strode the short distance to the truck and peered into the passenger-side window. When he tried the handle, it opened and he snorted.

"Idiot," I heard him mouth under his breath.

He stepped up to the inside of the truck, between the seat and the door. Instead of depositing me on the seat, he tightened his hold and looked down.

"The bad shit's over. I won't let him touch you again."

I nodded. His words loosened something inside me and made it easier to breathe. Gently, he placed me on the seat and then pulled back slightly. From this close, I could see the tenderness in his eyes, and then he pressed a kiss to my forehead.

When he climbed into the driver's seat, I glanced at the ignition. "There's no keys," I noted, nerves fluttering around in my chest.

"I don't need keys," he replied confidently.

I couldn't see what he was doing, but it sounded like he ripped out a part of the dash and then he shoved his hand up inside and pulled out a handful of wires.

"They teach you how to hotwire a car in the Marine Corps?" I asked incredulously.

He grinned. "Nope. I was a teenager once."

I couldn't help it. I smiled.

Then I glanced out the window. A familiar figure was rushing through the rain at us.

"Nathan," I cried, pointing in the direction of Lex.

The truck roared to life and he threw it in drive. The blast of a gun and the shattering of glass had me screaming.

"Get down," Nathan barked as he shoved at my head until I slid onto the floorboard.

I heard the truck accelerate and it fishtailed over the slick ground, but he didn't slow down. He ripped and roared down the side of the mountain until the gunshots couldn't even be heard in the distance.

18

Nathan

He shot out the back window. Holy shit, when that glass shattered and shards of it started raining from behind, I almost busted a vein. Honor was sitting right there. Right. Fucking. There.

If she'd have been shot or stabbed, I would have stopped the truck right then and killed him.

Bullets wouldn't have stopped me.

But the bullet didn't hit her, and as I tore down the mountain, I glanced toward the floorboard, expecting to see her spurting out red rain.

I never wanted to see that sight again.

But she wasn't bleeding. She didn't look hurt at all (well, no more than before).

"He's crazy!" she yelled over the rumble of the truck's engine as she gripped the edge of the seat while I flew around a curve. We came a little too close to going over the edge and plummeting down into the trees, so I laid off the gas.

Honor started to push herself up but then swore. I cut my eyes over to see a fresh trail of red sliding from the palm of her hand and winding a path down the inside of her wrist.

My stomach turned. The sight of blood didn't bother me, but the sight of it pouring from Honor's body did.

"Stay down," I said, averting my gaze. "There's too much glass up here."

But just because I wasn't looking didn't mean she stopped bleeding. With one hand, I reached around my neck and yanked the long-sleeve waffle-knit tee I was wearing over my head. I tossed it at her. "Here, wrap that around your hand."

"I don't want to ruin your shirt."

"You prefer blood loss?"

"I owe you a shirt with your pie," she said, and I smiled.

A few minutes later, I glanced back down at her hand, which was now completely covered with my shirt. She looked small, hunched down there on the floor. And pale. Her skin stood out against the darkness.

The reaction she had when she saw this truck wasn't good. I'd seen enough during my time in the Corps to know that something bad happened to her in this truck, something that her brain probably suppressed until she was brought face to face with it.

I felt like the world's biggest ass by forcing her into this vehicle. I was afraid to even know what the hell caused her to have such a violent reaction back there. But I didn't have a choice. This truck was our best option at getting away. It was beyond clear to me that Honor needed away from here as soon as possible.

Yeah, I wanted to stay and take him down.

Yeah, beating him in the head might feel good.

But the price of that would cost… maybe not cost someone like me anything, but it would cost Honor a lot. She'd already been through enough.

It was strange, the streak of protectiveness I felt when I looked at her. I'd never felt that way about anyone but my family and some of the men I worked with. But this was different… I'd only just met her. Why did I feel this innate drive to keep her safe?

It was almost as if something inside me claimed her.

The main road came into sight and my tense muscles relaxed a little.

"Where are we going?" Honor asked.

"I'm taking you to the hospital."

She groaned. "I want to go home."

"You need to be looked at. They'll give you something for those ribs."

"What about the police?"

"They can meet us at the hospital."

Honor was silent for a minute, and I knew her brain was working. I could almost hear her worry.

"You know his name? Where he lives?"

"Yeah, I do."

"You'll tell the police?"

I absolutely hated the tremor of fear in her voice. I knew she was worried he would come after her again. Hell, I was worried about that too.

"I'm gonna tell them, babe," I said, taking my eyes off the road and looking directly at her. "I'm going to tell them everything, and they're going to lock him up where he belongs."

She nodded and then rested her cheek against the thick shirt wrapped around her hand. The ride to the hospital was quiet. The closer we got, the more traffic surrounded us and the more relaxed I felt. I wondered what Lex was doing, how pissed he was that we left him stranded in the woods.

I pulled into the hospital. The whole place was lit up with bright lights. Ambulances lined the sidewalk beneath the awning for the ER entrance. They must've still been dealing with the car pileup from earlier tonight.

There were also some police cars with flashing lights parked at the curb. Good. That would make for easy contact.

Because it was so crowded near the entrance, I parked in the lot. Of course there was nothing available close. Every vacant space was in the nosebleed section, so I took the first spot I came to and then reached down low and disconnected the wires, shutting off the truck.

Honor still rested her cheek on her hands, her face turned away. I couldn't tell if she was asleep or not, but she didn't move even after I pushed open my door and got out. I went around to the passenger side and opened the door. I reached in and slid my arm around her waist, and this panicked sound ripped from her throat and her body went rigid.

Her head nearly smacked the glove compartment, but I blocked it with my hand.

"Easy," I said gently. "It's Nathan. We're at the hospital. Time to go inside."

Her body relaxed, but she made no move to get out. "I'm going to pick you up," I informed her. She didn't try to blacken my eye, so I took that as consent and lifted her out and then kicked the door closed.

Her cheek fell against my chest and her lips parted on a deep exhale. "I can walk," she protested.

I chuckled. She'd probably fall over the minute I put her down. "No," I said, leaving no room for argument. I wasn't about to admit how cute I thought she was. The minute she knew that, it would all be over. She'd have me wrapped around her little finger.

Ain't. Gonna. Happen.

I was going to place her in the doctors' care and then go talk to the police. Once that was done, so was my job. I could go home.

Go home to what? a voice in my head argued. *Cold fried chicken? Your weight set in the basement? Your memories?*

I ignored those thoughts as I walked past a police officer reclining against the side of his cruiser, holding a coffee cup in his hand. "I have a crime to report," I told him and kept walking.

He could follow me. It irritated me the way he was just standing there and Honor was out there dumped in a hole for fifteen hours. No, it wasn't that cop's fault, but… but I was irritated anyway.

Inside the ER I found what I expected. A lot of organized chaos. People filled the chairs with various injuries, all waiting to be seen. I clenched my jaw and went to the check-in desk.

"This woman needs to be seen. She was kidnapped, dumped in a hole, exposed to the elements, and has several broken ribs and various other injuries."

That got the nurse's attention. She stared at me and my bedraggled appearance with shock. "Who are you?"

Honor lifted her head off my chest and turned toward the woman, who gasped at the sight of her bruised and swollen face. "He's the guy who pulled me out of the hole. He's a Marine."

"Is she bleeding anywhere?" the nurse asked hopefully.

My back teeth came together.

"Yes," I ground out. Why did it matter?

Honor held up her hand wrapped in my shirt.

"When people come in bleeding, they get higher priority."

Oh. Well. That was good. "How long do we have to wait until she gets seen? She's been through a lot. She needs fluid and a bed."

She pushed a clipboard at me. "Sign in."

I signed in. Under my name. For some reason, having a record of her being here for anyone to see didn't sit well with me.

The nurse glanced up at me and then at Honor bundled up in my arms. Her eyes softened. "I'll see what I can do," she said low and then disappeared.

There wasn't an empty chair in this place. Not one.

I took up position against the wall, planted my feet, and tucked her a little closer to me. Honor seemed to be floating around somewhere between consciousness and sleep. It made me worry she had a concussion. She did have that bump on the back of her head.

Fifteen minutes later, the nurse from behind the desk motioned to me. I pushed away from the wall and followed her back along a quiet hallway and into a small area with a bed and a curtain all the way around it. "Someone will be in as soon as they can."

"Thank you," I told her, and I meant it.

She smiled and disappeared behind the curtain. Even though my arms were shaking with the effort of holding her for so long, I was hard pressed to put her down. I stood over the white bed for long minutes, debating, until I gently laid her out on the covers.

Her eyes fluttered open and she smiled. "Thanks."

"You look like shit," I told her tenderly and brushed a strand of damp hair off her face.

Her eyes widened and focused on my face. I opened my mouth to tell her I was teasing when she said, "There's lights in here."

Yeah. She hit her head too hard. "Yeah," I drawled slowly.

"I can see you." She said it like she was in awe.

"Well, I ain't much to look at." I started to pull away, but she grabbed my arm and yanked me back down so I was leaning over her body.

"Stay."

"I'm not going anywhere." I wasn't sure why I just said that, but it felt right.

Her eyes—a crystal-blue color—roamed over my face, taking in every feature, every scar I knew was there. I was probably unshaven, dirty, and looked like crap.

"You look…" she said, her voice trailing away as she looked me over again. I braced myself for some polite answer. But what she said surprised me. "Like a warrior."

I lifted my eyebrow. "A warrior, huh?"

She nodded. "Strong. Capable. Rough."

I grunted, not sure what to make of her words.

"I won't tell your secret," she said, a small smile playing on her lips.

"And what secret is that?" I asked, amused.

"That even though you look like a warrior and act like a warrior, underneath all that toughness is really a big mushy marshmallow."

I snorted. "There is nothing on me that resembles a marshmallow." I flexed my bicep for her to feast her eyes on.

She placed her palm over the center of my chest, right above my heart. All sense of joking totally left my body. I swallowed.

"It's why you need all those muscles, isn't it? To protect what's in here."

And *those* were the words that wrapped me right around her little finger.

19

Honor

I never thought I might actually enjoy being a patient at a hospital. Of course, when your options are that or death… being in a hospital scores a ten out of ten.

I didn't even mind the ugly gown they put me in because it meant finally getting out of my muddy, wet clothes. The IV hurt like hell, but whatever meds they put in it sure were nice. Finally, I could draw a breath without feeling like someone was stabbing me with a butcher knife.

The silence of the room was welcome. I liked silence. I knew some people who kept themselves so busy—their lives so full of all this… crap—that they never had a spare moment. I always felt bad for those people. It was almost as if they couldn't stand the thought of being at rest—of being alone with themselves.

Of course, even when I was alone and sitting in the silence of a room, I was never actually alone. The voices in my head—the characters that I put down on the page—they were always with me. It wasn't something I went around telling other people because they would likely put me in a padded room, but other writers understood. It was probably the reason I liked the silence so much, because then there was no exterior noise competing with the constant activity that went on within the confines of my brain.

Or maybe the silence was just welcome because it meant no one was throwing oranges at my head and trying to kill me.

I laid there as long as I could, ignoring reality, until I knew I couldn't ignore it any longer. I had to talk to the police. They needed to get that man off the streets. He could be doing to someone else what he'd just done to me.

My eyes sprang open.

I expected to see the curtain draped around the bed, but it wasn't there. In fact, I was no longer in the tiny cubicle that Nathan carried me into.

Nathan.

I turned my head, looking for him, but he wasn't there. I was in a room by myself, one of those generic hospital rooms that looked the same as every other in the building. White walls, cold tile floor, a rolling bedside table nearby, and a set of windows on the far end.

The curtains were drawn so I couldn't see outside, but judging from the amount of light in the room, I knew the sun was up. How long of a break from reality did I take?

I stared at the IV taped to the back of my hand and scowled. Stupid thing. As I pondered ripping it out, the door to the room opened and Nathan stepped inside.

He was still wearing the same white T-shirt and jeans he wore when he brought me in. They looked dry now but were wrinkled and covered in mud. It was the first time I really got a good look at him because it wasn't dark, it wasn't raining, and we weren't running from a madman.

Oh, and I guess the meds in the IV were making it easier to focus on him and not the pain.

I decided not to rip it out after all.

He was a big guy, over six feet tall, with a broad frame and very defined body. His biceps were large and hard. I probably wouldn't even be able to wrap my hand around them and let my fingers touch. His chest was also solid looking and the white shirt stretched across his pecs and lay smoothly over his flat stomach. Even his neck was thick, and I knew this was a man who spent a lot of time at the gym.

He saw I was awake and he strode to the end of the bed and stood, looking down at me. Usually, I hated people looming over me. It was creepy.

Nathan was not creepy.

His nearly black hair was super short, a typical military cut, I suppose. It graduated from being practically bald on the sides and faded upward to short strands on the top that were sticking up like he'd been running his hands over the top of his head.

He was also unshaven; dark, coarse hair covered the lower half of his face. I knew he most likely was always shaven, but his hair was so dark that the time he spent running around in the woods with me caused it to already shadow his jaw.

He had a strong nose with a little bump in the center (had it been broken?), dark thick eyebrows, and blue eyes. His skin wasn't as pale as mine, and he had a scar underneath his right eye. It ran jaggedly across his cheekbone. His lips were full, but there was also another scar right beneath his bottom lip, and it interrupted the curved line that his lips would have formed.

A black tattoo peaked out from under the sleeve on his left arm, and I began to daydream about what the entire tattoo looked like and if he had any more in places that were covered by his clothes.

"You're still here," I said, still not taking away my eyes.

"I told you I wouldn't leave."

He did say that, but I guess part of me thought he was only saying what he thought I wanted to hear. After all, I wasn't his responsibility. I mean, he barely knew me.

"How long was I out?"

He walked around the side of bed. I couldn't help but notice the way his hips swiveled as he moved. He dropped into a chair sitting right beside the bed and reclined against the back. "A couple hours."

"What time is it?"

"About ten a.m."

I felt my eyes widen. I'd been out more than a couple hours. He'd been here this whole time? "Aren't you exhausted?"

"Nah. I caught a couple hours of sleep."

"Where?"

"Right here."

He slept in the chair beside my bed? Damn if that didn't make my heart turn over.

"I should talk to the police." I started to push myself up.

He moved quickly, gently pressing me back down. "I already talked to them."

"You did?"

He nodded. "Yes. I gave them a description, his name, and his address."

Relief made me weak, and I leaned back against the pillow. "Did they arrest him?"

The area around Nathan's eyes became pinched. "Not yet."

Well, this wasn't good. "Why not?"

"They're still looking for him."

"Where is he?" I demanded.

"We aren't sure. They've got men out in the woods where you were. He's just… gone."

"They believe us, right?" I worried. What if they thought I was lying? What if no one believed us? He would just get away with what he did.

"Yes, Honor, they believe us. They found the hole you were in."

My stomach tightened at the thought of that nasty hole. I had another thought that had me sitting up quickly. My head swam, but I ignored it. "The necklace!"

"I gave it to them." He reassured me. "I showed them the picture you texted me too."

"What was her name?" I whispered. I needed to know the name of the girl who wasn't as lucky as I was.

He frowned. "Honor—"

"Her name," I said firmly, cutting off whatever protest he was about to spew.

"Mary."

I was silent while the name sank in. The horrors she must have experienced in her final hours of life were things no woman should ever have to endure. Memories of the truck, of my kidnapper pinning me down and putting his… his… parts in my face assaulted me.

I squeezed my eyes closed, willing away the images.

"Hey," Nathan said, and I felt the bed dip beneath his weight. "What's going on in there?" I felt his finger tap my forehead.

I opened my eyes and stared into his blue irises. "How do you forget?" I whispered.

He knew what I meant. I could see it on his face. It was the kind of understanding that told me he too had experienced things that would forever leave a mark on his soul.

He trailed the backs of his knuckles over my cheek and then tucked my hair behind my ear. "You don't," he said gently. "You just have to find a way to live with it and go on."

"Will it get easier?"

I saw the war wage in his eyes. He wanted to tell me yes. He wanted to take away some of what I was feeling. But Nathan was no liar; that much I knew to the deepest places within me. He wasn't the kind of man to sugarcoat something that couldn't be sweetened.

"I don't know, baby," he said gently. "I sure hope so."

My chest felt tight and my stomach was jittery. Hearing such tenderness out of this large and steely man did things—*very good things*—to my body.

It was the stuff I wrote about.

The stuff I never really thought existed outside of those pages.

My fingers itched; they longed to touch him. He was so close, and he watched me so carefully that I couldn't resist slowly reaching out to trace along the jagged scar that stretched across his cheekbone. He didn't flinch or pull away. He sat there completely still while my fingers caressed him.

"What happened to you?" I whispered.

He caught my fingers and pulled them away, wrapping his around mine, dwarfing my hand in his, and pulled it close to his chest. I waited for his answer, curious and patient at the same time. I knew whatever answer he would give would not come easy, and I didn't mind waiting. Nathan was a man worth waiting for.

The door made a loud scraping sound as it opened and dragged across the floor. Irritation skittered through me because someone dared to interrupt this moment. I didn't want anyone else in here. I only wanted Nathan.

Get a grip, I told myself. *This isn't some cheesy soap opera. This is real life. You got shit to do.*

But even my thoughts couldn't keep my eyes from straying from him.

"Miss Calhoun," an older doctor in a white coat said. "Glad to see you're awake." He carried a clipboard (didn't they always?) and had the traditional stethoscope hung around his neck.

"How are you feeling?" the doctor asked as Nathan released my hand and returned to his chair beside the bed.

"I'm fine, thank you."

"The police are here. They would like to take your statement."

Nathan sat up a little higher in his chair but said nothing. I nodded. "That's fine. I'm sorry I slept so long."

"Your body needed the rest, Miss Calhoun. We gave you something to help you sleep. From here on out, you will be getting Naproxen, which is similar to a strong Motrin."

I nodded.

"Are you in pain?"

"A little," I admitted. "But it's not as bad as before."

The doctor glanced at the clipboard. "Most of your injuries are superficial and will heal quickly. You have a lot of bruising, some swelling, and a bump on your head. It doesn't appear that you have a concussion. We put three stitches in your hand and removed the glass that was beneath the skin."

I glanced down at my hand, which was bandaged. How had I not realized I had stitches until he pointed it out? It must have been from the glass in the truck.

"Our biggest concern is your ribs." The doctor continued.

"They're broken," I said. It wasn't a question.

"Yes. Several of them. You appear to have suffered blunt force trauma to your torso area."

"He kicked me," I reiterated.

The doctor cleared his throat. "You have heavy bruising, swelling, and mild tissue damage. Have you ever had a broken rib before?"

"No." I'd never had a broken bone at all.

"It's quite painful. There really is no treatment for a broken rib, just pain management, which is what the Naproxen is for. Years ago, doctors used compression bandages to treat broken ribs, but its since been deemed unsafe. You see, the risks of having broken ribs is that you're at a high risk for pneumonia."

Pneumonia? That was weird.

"She was out in the rain, in the cold, all night," Nathan said.

"I'm aware," the doctor replied. "So far, you show no signs of becoming ill."

"But why pneumonia?" I asked.

"Because when you suffer that kind of trauma, it prevents you from taking deep breaths. This increases your risk. If you begin to run a fever, feel weak or dizzy, or experience any other worrisome symptoms, you need to seek medical treatment immediately."

"Okay, I will."

"I'll send the police in now," he said after a few more moments of talking. When he finally left, I blew out a breath.

"Doctor's are so serious," I mumbled.

Nathan chuckled. "Would you rather he be unserious?"

"I want to go home," I griped.

He grinned.

Two police officers shuffled into the room, wearing pressed uniforms with badges clipped to their black belts. Resigned, I submitted to their questions and prying eyes. Because Nathan filled them in so thoroughly, their questions turned personal fast.

"Did Lex Sullman rape you, ma'am?"

I recoiled like I smelled something foul.

"What the hell kind of question is that?" Nathan said, jerking up from his chair and taking up position beside the bed.

"A necessary one," the police replied, gauging Nathan, no doubt taking in his rough appearance and scars. His eyes slid to me. "How do you know this man?"

"I already told you that," he said, and I knew he was restraining his temper. Nathan seemed to have a bit of a short fuse.

Before things could escalate, I explained quickly about how Nathan and I met.

"So you are friends with the man suspected of kidnapping women?"

"No," Nathan said slowly, like he was talking to an idiot. "Like I told you before, we play a weekly poker game together. He's an acquaintance."

"You provided us with his home address." The other officer spoke up.

Nathan shrugged. "I've played poker at his house."

"Will other men testify to this?"

Nathan rattled off about four names and a phone number of some guy named Patton. When he was done, the muscle in the side of his jaw was ticking. It reminded me of a time bomb ready to explode.

"No," I said quietly.

All eyes turned toward me.

"No?" the officer asked.

"He didn't rape me."

Nathan dropped onto the bed beside me. It was as if he was so relieved he couldn't stand. I gave him a watery smile.

The police officer looked at his partner. "We're not looking for a rapist." The other partner nodded and wrote something in a no-nonsense black notebook.

They said it like it somehow made everything I'd gone through okay. Like what I suffered was somehow less now because my body wasn't violated like they assumed.

It really, really made me angry.

This wasn't just about me. It was also about Mary and whoever else came before us. "He was going to," I said, and once again all eyes turned to me.

"How do you know that?"

"He made his intent pretty clear," I hedged.

Nathan was sitting very still and staring at the floor. I glanced at him, feeling unease curling through my limbs.

"Maybe you should wait outside, Mr. Reed."

"No," I said, reaching for his hand. I didn't want him to go. This was hard enough to say out loud. Knowing Nathan was here and that he somehow understood something about pain made it easier.

Before the officers could insist, I opened my mouth and let it pour out. "He held me down," I said. "He... um... he took himself out." I paused, looking at the officers, hoping they would understand. Both of them wore a disgusted look so I knew they understood perfectly. "And he tried to shove it in my mouth."

Nathan glanced at me. "The truck?" he whispered, harsh.

I nodded.

He ripped his hand from mine and hooked it around the back of my head, pulling me into his chest. He still smelled like pine trees, and I let it fill my senses.

"Is that all?" one of the officers asked.

I lifted my head, anger on my face. "Well, aside from being kicked, slapped, punched, shot at, groped, and thrown into a thirty-foot hole in the ground, I guess that about covers it."

"We meant no disrespect," the second officer spoke.

"Yeah, I know." I relented.

"I think we have all we need for now. We'll leave a card. If you remember anything else, please contact us."

"Wait," I called. "Did you find him? Is he in jail?"

The officers exchanged a long look. I knew what that meant.

"I'm afraid the suspect is still at large."

Why did they keep calling him the "suspect?" He was frickin' guilty as sin. "You have to find him," I implored.

"The department is doing everything we can, ma'am."

"It isn't enough!" I shouted.

"We'll let you know when we've apprehended the—"

"Suspect." I spat the word for him. I hoped he realized how disgusted I was by the police department's incompetence.

He had the grace to flush as the second officer let himself out the door. Before following behind, he turned back and cleared his throat. "I should probably caution you, ma'am," he began. "You need to remain precautious and alert until he is in custody."

I nodded, the hair on the back of my neck rising just a little.

And then I was alone with Nathan. I looked at him. "What a bunch of idiots," I muttered. "If you hadn't found me, I'd probably be dead by now. They certainly wouldn't have found me."

He grimaced. "I had to show them where the hole was."

I covered my mouth with my hand and giggled. It was terrible, but if I couldn't laugh, I might start screaming. The sudden burst of laughter caused me to wince in pain.

"Easy," Nathan cautioned, placing a hand on my shoulder and pressing me back in the bed. "You need to rest."

How the heck was I supposed to rest when *that man* was still out there?

20

Nathan

I spent the night watching her sleep. Sometimes I saw her face twist in fear and pain; sometimes I would hear a low whimper.

I knew that sound, and I imaged my face likely looked a lot like hers—except much uglier—when I slept. I was thankful for the meds in her IV because I knew once she got home, she wouldn't get much rest.

Nightmares would likely plague her.

The police were a bunch of idiots. They had no idea how to talk to people who'd been through hell. They had no idea how to search the woods. Shit, I had to leave the hospital and drive out there to *show* them where the hole was.

It made me angry. Leaving her lying there, all black and blue, with her face in a permanent grimace, was surprisingly hard. It was only after I made sure a police officer stayed behind that I left for the mountain.

Where I got angry all over again.

When I first found Honor, she hadn't been in the hole. Lex pulled her up. The rope ladder was still lying in a heap on the ground. One of the officers shined a large light down into the hole… and I felt sick. It was a muddy, dark pit. *She spent fifteen hours down there.* The thought replayed over and over in my mind until I had to turn away.

Even still, the sight remained. The rain finally stopped but had come down so hard there were several inches of water just sitting stagnant at the bottom. It was likely ice cold. He would have left her down there to freeze, to fear, and then he planned to come back to kill her.

Maybe it was a good thing the cops couldn't find him. He was safer that way. Of course, his safety was the very last thing I cared about.

Once I showed them the scene of the crime and answered a million other questions *and* showed them my Wrangler with the ruined tires, I finally went back to the hospital where I took up residence beside her bed.

It really wasn't that uncomfortable. I'd slept in worse places.

She was being released from the hospital soon, and the police still hadn't brought in Lex. They weren't going to. Enough time passed that he was likely long gone or in a place no one knew about, plotting out some sick plan.

It was hard to say. People who weren't right in the head were very unpredictable. I glanced at Honor, who wasn't doing a very good job of resting.

I wouldn't rest easy, either, if I were her. She was basically a sitting duck.

"You don't have to stay, you know," Honor said, turning her head to the side to look directly at me. "You've already done so much. If it wasn't for you—"

I held up my hand to halt her words. "Don't say it," I replied.

A smile played on her lips and a mischievous little light came into her eyes. "Say what?" she asked innocently. "That you look like you need a shower?"

I glanced down at my rumpled clothes and muddy boots. "So you're picturing me naked over there?" I quipped. "Here I thought the reason you seemed so anxious was because you wanted out of here." I sat forward, bringing my face closer to hers. "If you wanted to see me naked, you should have just asked."

She actually blushed. But even embarrassment wasn't enough to keep her mouth shut. "Oh please," she said and rolled her eyes. "Do those corny lines actually work on women?"

I grinned and sat back. "I don't know."

Her eyes narrowed. "You don't know?"

"Nope."

She pursed her lips. "Do they work on men?"

I laughed out loud.

"What?" She shrugged. "I watch the news. I heard all about how the military lifted the 'don't ask, don't tell' policy." She leaned closer to me like she was telling me a secret. I wanted to grab her face and kiss the shit out of her. "I can legally ask you that now."

Then she actually wagged her eyebrows at me.

I bit back a smile and leaned forward once again. Our faces were mere inches apart and our lips were lined up for a kiss...

"I'm not gay," I whispered.

"No judgment here," she said. "I need a good shopping buddy."

Honor moved to sit back, but I gently grasped her wrist and pulled her back. "I'm not gay," I repeated again, my voice even lower, as my mouth hovered oh so close to hers.

Everything about her stilled. Her little pink tongue darted out and wet her bottom lip, which was still just slightly swollen from whatever happened to it. I'd never been so insanely tempted to lick someone as I was now.

"You're not?" she whispered.

I shook my head and leaned a fraction closer. "Nope. I'm willing to prove it."

She made a small sound in the back of her throat, kind of like a purr. I liked that sound. I liked it a hell of a lot.

I let our lips hang there, almost touching, drawing out the anticipation of the kiss... Usually, I would instantly go for it, but this was different. Honor was different. I wanted a chance to feel every single thing. Every ounce of desire, every single thread of anticipation. She wasn't something I wanted to hurry up and get over with; she wasn't something I wanted to use to pass the time or to make me forget.

I wanted more than that from Honor.

I wasn't sure why.

Or how.

But I knew down to my bones that didn't make it any less true.

Just when I couldn't take the distance any longer, the door to the room opened. We sprang apart, looking at each other with a little bit of shock and disappointment written on both our faces.

"Honor!" called a woman from just inside the door.

"Mom," Honor replied, finally looking away from me and toward the woman moving into the room.

She wasn't a large woman, maybe five feet four, with chin-length dark hair and brown eyes. She wore a pair of loose, black knit pants with a long-sleeved white T-shirt and a red zippered fleece vest. "Thank God you're okay," she said, setting a medium-sized multicolored bag on the end of the bed. She placed her hands on her hips and studied Honor and all her bruises. "You should have called earlier, young lady."

Honor rolled her eyes. "I was a little busy, Mom."

"You've been here all night," she replied, still gazing at her daughter steadily.

I didn't really care for her tone.

I cleared my throat. "She's been medicated. She just woke up a while ago."

Her mother turned to me. "Are you the one that pulled her out of that hole?"

My lips itched to smile. "Technically, she was already out of it when I found her."

"You're a Marine?"

"Yes, ma'am." I stood, holding out my hand. "My name is Nathan Reed. Nice to meet you."

Her mother slid a cool hand into mine and shook it firmly. "How much food does someone like you eat?"

"*Mother,*" Honor admonished.

Honor's mother turned toward her daughter. "What?" she asked like it was a perfectly reasonable question. "He's huge."

I grinned. "I like pie."

Her mother looked at me. "What kind of pie?"

"Apple," Honor answered.

I grinned wider.

Her mother looked between me and her daughter. Then she hugged me. It caught me off guard, and I looked over her head at Honor, who seemed to be just as shocked as I was.

I wasn't sure what to do so I patted her back awkwardly. She pulled away and looked up. "Call me Mom. Welcome to the family."

Honor made a strangled sound in the back of her throat. I didn't say anything at all. I was too busy feeling like all the wind was knocked out of me.

"Mom" acted like she hadn't just shocked everyone in the room silent and grabbed the bag she put on the bed. "I stopped by your house and got you some clothes and some shampoo." She gave Honor a long look and then said, "I should have brought conditioner."

Honor laughed. "What will the nurses say?" She gasped and put her hand to her mouth.

To my surprise, her mother's eyes filled with tears, and then she hugged Honor. I knew the power that her slight arms were capable of, and I winced thinking of Honor's ribs. Over her mother's shoulder, I saw the look of pain register, but she didn't say a word.

"I'm just going to go unpack what you need in the bathroom," Mom said, taking the bag and disappearing in the adjoining bathroom.

She shut the door behind her.

Honor and I looked at each other. "Her name is Mona."

"She told me to call her Mom." I smirked.

"She must like you."

"How about you?" I said, sitting down on the edge of the bed before I could stop myself. "Do you like me?"

She shrugged. "You're okay."

"Just okay, huh?"

She wrinkled her nose. "Eh," she said.

If her ribs weren't broken, I would've tickled her until she changed her answer. I settled for just looking at her, taking in her rough appearance. Even still, she was beautiful. I couldn't imagine how much more so she would be when all the leaves were out of her hair and her eye was no longer swollen shut.

The atmosphere around us changed, becoming charged, more electric. The pull I felt to her was undeniable, kind of like I was an alcoholic and she was my favorite drink. Except alcohol wasn't a very good habit...

I had a feeling Honor would be very, very good.

The sound of something being dropped echoed through the wall by the bathroom. Without taking my eyes off Honor, I said, "I should probably go."

Tension crept into her features, tightening her lips and creating a barely there wrinkle between her eyes. "I'm sure you want to shower."

"Showering is overrated."

She smiled.

Her smile did things to me... made me feel lighter somehow. Like all the sticky cobwebs of the past were being swept away. "I'm not leaving here without your number."

I wasn't sure, but it seemed some of the tension in her face eased.

"You got something to write on?"

I glanced around the room. There wasn't even a pen in sight. "I'll get something from the nurse."

Her mother was coming out of the bathroom when I left the room, going in search of a pen. I didn't really want to leave, but it seemed like I shouldn't stay either. Technically, I wasn't anyone to Honor. The only reason the nurses let me in the room at all to begin with was because I was the one who brought her in... and because I can be damn intimidating when I want to be and no one dared tell me to leave.

But now her mother was here. She was being discharged and would likely go and stay with her family where she would be cared for and safe. There was nothing left for me to do... but go home.

To an empty house.

The thought twisted my stomach, but I told myself to man up. At least she was giving me her number. I would call her. I would ask her out.

Honor didn't know it yet, but she was about to become a fixture in my life.

21

Honor

"Is he leaving?" Mom asked, watching as Nathan pulled the door around behind him.

My stomach was all kinds of discombobulated. That man had an effect on me like no other. I felt breathless every time he got close, and it wasn't because my ribs were broken.

"He's coming back," I said, "which is a shock after the way you just acted."

"Posh." She scoffed (in the language of my mother, that meant she thought I was being silly). "That man is so taken with you he probably didn't even notice I was talking."

"Mom," I groaned. "This isn't some matchmaking opportunity." My mother had a very bad habit of trying to fix me up with every single eligible bachelor she met. It didn't matter if she knew him or not. One time she tried to set me up with our waiter when we went out to dinner.

She was positively relentless. But I loved her anyway.

"I don't have to play matchmaker," Mom said, sitting down in the chair Nathan just abandoned. He made the chair look small, but with her sitting there, it looked a lot larger. "The vibes between you two were rippling through this room the minute I walked in."

"The vibes?" I said, thinking her colorful vocabulary was likely the reason I became a writer.

"You know," she said, wagging her eyebrows. "The mojo."

I burst out laughing. It hurt and I collapsed against the pillow.

Mom started fluttering around, trying to adjust my pillow. When the pillow didn't fluff up to her liking, she frowned. "Go get cleaned up so we can go. The pillows at home are much more comfortable."

She didn't mean my house. My home. "Mom," I said gently. "You know I'm going to my house, right?"

She looked at me like I had three heads. I admit, my eye was swollen enough that I probably looked like I had two. "You are *not* going home alone, young lady," she said in a stern, no-nonsense voice.

"Yes, I am."

"Shall I call your father?"

"I'm not twelve. That threat doesn't work on me anymore."

"Posh," she said again and dug around in her too-large bag and pulled out a cell phone. "I'm calling him," she said, giving me one last chance to change my mind.

Nathan walked in the room, carrying a pen and a small piece of white paper.

"Go ahead," I told her.

She pressed a few buttons and then paced over to the window. A few seconds later, my father must have answered because she said, "Eric, you need to give this girl a talking to!"

Then she launched into some tirade, which she tried to whisper like she was being secretive. I looked at Nathan and rolled my eyes.

"What's going on?" he asked, coming closer.

"She's mad because I told her I wouldn't come and stay with her."

He frowned. "You should."

"Not you too."

"You shouldn't be alone right now." The way he said it made me think he had some reasons.

I knew what those reasons were. It was exactly why I couldn't stay with my mother.

I sighed. "Look, you and I both know he's still out there. What if he finds me?"

"He can't find you if you aren't home."

"He doesn't know my address."

Nathan rolled his eyes. "Have you ever heard of the Internet?"

"I can't put my parents in danger," I said low.

He pressed his lips together. I knew he understood. Still, he protested. "Your safety matters too."

He was right; it did matter. But I honestly thought I would be safe at home. Lex didn't even know my name. Finding my address would be very hard if he didn't know who he was looking for. Unless, of course, if he read paranormal and romance novels, which I highly doubted.

"I will be safe. At home. I'll be comfortable there too," was all I said. God, how I craved the quiet comfort of being at home.

"I don't like this."

"It's not your decision."

He didn't like that too well. I could read it on his face. He said nothing else but thrust the paper before me and handed me the pen.

I scrawled my number across the top.

"I want your address too," he said when I tried to hand it back.

"Why?" I scowled.

"I'm nosy."

"I'm private."

"I'll join sides with your mother if you don't write it down."

Well, damn. Then I would never get any peace. "Fine." I wrote down my address.

Nathan took the paper and read it over. Then he tore off the blank bottom section of the paper and wrote something on it and handed it to me. "Here's my number. You can call me. Anytime. Night or day."

"I thought it had water damage, you know, from the rain?"

"I took the battery out when we got here and let the pieces dry. It's working now."

"That's good," I said, glancing down at the number again. "Thanks." I looked at my mother, who was still talking animatedly to my father. It was a good time for me to escape. "I'm going to go shower."

I glanced down at my hands. One was taped up where the IV had been and the other was wrapped, covering my stitches.

Showering likely was going to be a challenge.

"Need some help?" Nathan said, giving me a roguish grin.

I laughed. "You wish." I pushed back the covers and the air brushed over my bare legs. I hoped my mother brought warm clothes because I seriously wanted to bundle up. And I desperately wanted some coffee. With cinnamon creamer.

Yum.

Nathan stepped back as I flung my legs over the side of the mattress and sat up. My ribs protested and I wasn't looking forward to moving around or seeing the black and blue marks all over my body once I was naked.

They were only ugly reminders of what I just went through.

Bruises fade. It's the internal damage you need to watch out for. The inner thought caused me to stumble a little as I stood.

But I didn't fall. Nathan was there to steady me. His hands caught me around the hips, supporting me, as his pine scent whirled around us. I probably smelled like dirty butt, but he smelled delicious. So unfair.

"You doing okay?" Nathan murmured close to my ear before straightening up to look at me. He kept his hands at my waist.

I nodded.

"Come on," he said gently. "I'll help ya." The southern drawl to his voice washed over me. It was like balm to an open wound. Like music notes to a song.

Yeah, okay, I could have made it to the bathroom all by myself. Still, I leaned into him just a little bit more.

You would have too.

He was so much bigger than me, something I hadn't paid much attention to when we were on the mountain. My body had always been aware of him, but not like this. It was as if the more I was around him the more hyperaware my nerves became.

When we reached the bathroom door, he used one arm to push it open and hold it there while I walked ahead. I glanced back at my mother, and she was no longer talking to my father. She stood there watching us, smiling, while holding the phone pressed to her ear.

Yet another reason I had to go home. She was going to be relentless on insisting that Nathan and I were soul mates or some such crap like that. I was the writer, but my mother had always been a dreamer.

"Lace," Nathan said, staring at the panties my mother displayed on top of the sink. I swear if I hadn't known any better I would have thought she did it on purpose.

I felt my face blush as I took in the light-peach lace panties with the lavender bow at the front. I wasn't about to grab them and hide them. Like I told my mother, I wasn't twelve.

I tried to think of what one of the kickass heroines in my novels would do. Hell, they would probably tuck the tiny fabric into his jeans pocket and tell him to keep them.

I wasn't that bold.

And I wasn't about to go commando.

Talk about uncomfortable.

"Looking at a lady's panties is impolite," I told him, taking in the shower stall with the safety bars all around.

"I never claimed to have any manners."

Well, if that didn't send heat pooling into my nether regions and make me think of all the naughty things a man like him could come up with… I blushed again.

He chuckled. "Turn around."

"What?" I asked dumbly.

"Turn around so I can untie your gown."

"Uhhh…"

"Relax, I might not have any manners, but I sure as hell have respect." He reached around me and felt for the tie between my shoulder blades. He found it and tugged the string as he spoke. "Figured it might be uncomfortable to reach around this far up."

Oh, well, yeah. "Thanks," I said, feeling a little bit of air brush over my back.

"You're set on going home, huh?" he asked after he pulled away.

I nodded. I wasn't going to change my mind. I didn't want anyone else in danger because some crazed asshole was after me. And I wanted to be home, in my own bed, in my own house with my own coffee creamer.

"Can I call you, Honor?" His voice brushed over me like a caress.

"I gave you my number,"

"Give me permission to use it."

"I thought you didn't have any manners," I countered, smiling.

He stroked a finger along my jawline. My entire body turned to Jell-O. "I want to hear you say it."

I didn't hear my voice when I spoke. I couldn't hear anything over the thudding of my heart. "You can call me, Nathan."

He gently hooked his hand around the back of my head and stepped closer. His lips pressed against my forehead and stayed there for long, blissful seconds. Too soon, he released me and I had to steady myself by gripping the counter.

"If you need me, call."

I nodded.

"I mean it. I'll always come if you need me."

"What if you're in the middle of hot steamy sex?" I burst out. Then I gasped. What the hell was I thinking?

Oh, wait. I wasn't. My damn hormones had taken over.

A slow smile spread across his face. "You won't need the phone, then, sweetheart, because you'll be the one beneath me."

I stared at him dumbly, unable to reply. After one long, heated look, he turned and left the bathroom, closing the door behind him.

The second he was gone, I collapsed against the sink in a flurry of heat and desire.

22

Nathan

I hated the quiet. It was too loud.

Meaning it made it way to convenient for the memories, for the ghosts, to come out and play.

It was going to be quiet when I got home tonight.

I decided not to go home right away. I called Patton while I was still at the hospital and he came to pick me up. I knew he would ask me questions, but I needed a ride and help with my Wrangler. I was waiting outside when he pulled up in his black Dodge Ram. On the back window was a giant Marine Corps decal sporting the eagle, globe, and anchor that made up the emblem of the Corps.

I glanced at the sky as I climbed into the truck. It was gloomy and gray, the clouds were heavy with rain, and I hoped that it held off for a while. The wind was brisk and chilly. It got cold here, and it got cold fast. I wasn't used to this type of chill so early in the fall. I was a true southern boy, and where I came from, we didn't even turn off our air-conditioning until it was almost November.

My fleece was still with Honor and my thermal had gone right in the trash. Blood didn't wash out very well. And even if it had, I would never wear that shirt again. I could never wear something that Honor had bled all over; just being reminded of it would make me angry.

"Thanks for the ride," I told Patton as I shut the door against the autumn wind.

"Sure thing, man. What's going on?"

"You got anything going on in the next couple hours?" I asked, not yet answering his question.

"Nope."

"No lady waiting for you at your place?"

He grinned. "You know me." He flashed a smile as he pulled into traffic. "No strings attached."

Patton liked women. But he hated commitment.

I understood that. Hell, I was that way too. Being in the Corps was hard on a relationship. The saying I heard many times was "if the Marines wanted you to have a wife, they would have issued you one in boot camp." In other words, the job came first. A lot of families suffered for that. A lot of failed marriages. A lot of infidelity. It was hard to hold a family together when you were never home.

Marines worked long hours. Hard hours. We trained. We deployed. The job followed us home… There was no "off" time for a Marine. Our jobs didn't end at five o'clock, and the wives—the other half of the relationship—were oftentimes left handling everything on their own.

Was it fair? Nope.

Did we get paid enough? Excuse me while I laugh.

It seemed easier just to stay single. Some days it was hard enough worrying about myself without adding someone else to the list.

But all that was before Honor.

Now I understood why some men married, why some men got out early, and why some men actually wanted to go home and not work late.

"My Jeep's sitting up on the mountain with two busted tires. I need to swing by the house, get an extra spare, and then go out there and change them so I can drive it home."

Patton nodded. "No problem."

That was the good thing about being a Marine. Even miles and miles away from home, I still had family that would be there when I needed something.

"So," Patton began, sliding me a glance. "You gonna tell me why your Jeep's jacked up, why you look like hell, and why you called me about Lex last night?"

"It all started with a girl," I said.

Patton grinned. "Hell yeah, all the best trouble starts with a girl."

I laughed. "Actually, it started with a text…"

It took the entire drive to my house and to the Wrangler for me to tell him everything. Then while we changed the tires, he asked me about a million questions. I answered them all, rattling off the information almost on autopilot as my thoughts drifted to Honor. By now she would be home. Alone.

Unless of course her mother—that woman was a piece of work—managed to strong-arm her to come home with her. I doubted that though… Honor didn't seem like the type to be strong armed into doing anything.

"Reed," Patton said from above.

I glanced up. He was standing there looking at me with a weird expression on his face. "What?"

"Dude, you got it bad."

"Got what?" I said as I finished tightening the last of the lug nuts.

"She must be hot," he said with a smirk.

I didn't really like him talking about her. At all. "She's not one of your one-night stands," I said, giving the nuts one last tightening.

He chuckled. "She gonna be one of yours?"

I dropped the lug wrench on the ground and stood. "Since some sicko that we played poker with tried to jam his cock down her throat, I would say trying to get in her pants would be a little shitty. Even for me," I spat.

Patton swore. "He in jail?"

"Stupid cops can't find him."

"We need to do a little recon on our own?"

"It's definitely an option."

"I'm up for it. Hell, half the guys in the unit would be all over this. We'd get him in less than twenty-four hours."

"I'll think about it," I said.

We gathered up the tools and threw the ruined tires in the bed of Patton's truck as thunder began to rumble overhead. It reminded me of just last night, how I was running through this very wood, trying to get Honor the hell out of there.

It also reminded me of gunfire.

"Hey," Patton said as I dug my keys out of pocket.

"Yeah?"

"You know I didn't mean nothing earlier. I was just kidding. I might have a lot of one-night stands, but I respect women. I would never—"

"Yeah, man. I know." I clapped him on the back. "I'm just pissed off."

"You got a right to be."

"Thanks for giving me a hand. Beer's on me next time."

Patton nodded. "You know you saved her life, right?"

After that we parted ways.

As I drove home, I wondered if saving her life made up for the one I wasn't able to save.

23

Honor

I liked the quiet. But today it was too silent.

Usually, the characters that lived in my head, the unseen worlds where I seemed to exist kept me occupied the entire day.

Today, those characters were inaudible. The worlds were hushed. It was almost as if they stayed away because they knew I wouldn't be able to deal with them and reality. I needed a break from reality. I wanted the voices back.

I smiled to myself as I wandered down the hallway and into my bedroom. I should call the doctor and ask him where the voices went. In my room, I drifted over to one of the windows that overlooked the trail. Burnished orange leaves fell from the trees and floated down onto the gravel walkway.

I felt the familiar tug I always did to go out there and walk, to breathe in deeply of the crisp air. I turned away from the sight. It might be beautiful, it might be peaceful out there… but sometimes looks were deceiving. The last time I was out there I was taken. Violated. Hurt.

I padded across the light-colored carpet and tugged open the white closet doors on the other side of the room. My clothes hung neatly and sat in folded stacks. I selected my favorite pair of black leggings and an oversized gray shirt with dolman sleeves. My father always said this shirt made me look like I had wings.

If I had wings today, I might fly away.

Even though I showered at the hospital, I took off the jeans and sweater my mother brought me and tossed them across the foot of my queen-sized bed. It was still neatly made from yesterday. The white comforter remained tucked tidily around the mattress and the earth-colored pillows were strategically placed the way I liked them.

I went into the bathroom, wincing at the coldness of the tile floor against my bare feet. I thought about showering again, I wanted to, but I didn't want the hassle of trying to keep my stitches dry. Instead, I used a fluffy white cloth to wash my face (one handed) at the sink and then I applied a really yummy smelling, rich lotion to my poor battered skin.

It was the first time I really looked at myself since being kidnapped. Yeah, there was a mirror in the bathroom at the hospital, but I avoided it. I wasn't ready to see. But being home made me feel a little stronger.

The swelling around my eye wasn't as bad as I knew it was before. My vision was a lot less impaired now. It was still puffy and sore looking. The bruise was a deep purple shade that no makeup was going to cover. It circled around my entire eye, making me look like a raccoon. My lower lip was partially swelled as well. It was also bruised, but it was small and already yellowing. There were various scrapes across my cheeks, likely from all the times I fell and hit my face against the ground.

At least I didn't look incredibly pale… All the injuries were too colorful for that.

My midsection looked the worst. The entire side of my ribs was black and blue. It also appeared lumpy and it made me recoil. From what the doctor said, it would be a while for them to heal. I was going to be stiff and sore, breathing was going to be a pain, and I was just going to have to live with it.

I would rather live with broken ribs than be dead.

The scrapes across my knuckles were only partially visible because gauze was wrapped around the stitches. I knew I could take off the wrapping, but I wasn't ready for that yet. I'd rather keep the stitches covered. The skin on the back of my other hand was itchy and a little tingly.

I soaked the tape in a little bit of warm water and then peeled it off. It hurt, but the relief of having that crappy medical tape off me was worth it. My skin was angry and red where it had been and there was a red rash covering the area. In the center was a bruise, and I wondered if the nurse had been careful at all when she jammed the IV into my hand.

My hair was in a simple braid and I let it loose, shaking the waves around my shoulders. I liked the way it felt when the ends of my hair brushed over my bare shoulders. After I brushed my teeth, I pulled on the leggings and shirt and added a pair of slippers that looked like boots.

I put on a pot of coffee and waited in the kitchen for it to drip enough for me to fill a mug, and I added some of my favorite cinnamon-flavored creamer. The first sip was heaven. It was like a warm blanket for my insides. Just holding the warmth of the mug between my chilled fingers was comforting.

I let out a contented sigh and then carried my mug out into the living room where I settled with a blanket on the couch.

I picked up my Kindle and turned it on, calling up the newest book I was reading by Jennifer Armentrout, and then sat it in my lap. Vivid images of Lex scattered my concentration and took away whatever peace I'd managed to find.

Maybe I shouldn't have let my mother go home after all. Maybe I should have asked her to stay. Maybe I should have given in and went home with her.

I could call her. She would come. Or my father would.

Instead, I clicked on the TV and found some old romantic comedy that always seemed to be playing. I knew I should pull up my social media. I likely had hundreds of notifications, messages, and emails to go through.

But what was I supposed to say?

Sorry I haven't been around. I almost died. I was kidnapped and the man who did it is still out there.

No computer for me today. I wasn't ready to deal with anything. I drank my coffee and stared at the TV for a long time, but I didn't really pay attention.

I wondered about Mary. About what the police told her family when I gave them the locket. I wondered if they changed her case from missing person to search and recovery. I knew she was dead. I hated it. I knew that she likely suffered horribly before she died. I hated that too.

Where was the justice for Mary? For any of his victims?

Was there a punishment worthy of such a heinous crime?

Death seemed too easy. Sitting in jail didn't seem like enough either. I asked myself what a fitting penance was for a man who tortured women.

A little while later, I forced myself to eat some toast and I drank more coffee. My eyes kept going to my laptop, but I never turned it on. My dad called to make sure I was okay, and my mother got on the line to see if I changed my mind about coming home.

I told her I was already home.

Then I promised I would come over the next day to visit.

At eight o'clock, I crawled into bed, leaving on the bathroom light. I was exhausted, but it took a while to fall asleep.

I was running on the trail, the sun filtering through the trees and the sound of water rushing through the river at my side. I wasn't running because I wanted to, though. I was scared. My heart beat frantically and fear seized my body. As I ran, I looked over my shoulder, so afraid that he'd caught up. He was there, but I was still just out of his reach. I told myself to go faster, to get the hell away, but I felt like my feet were encased in concrete.

"The cat always catches the mouse," the voice behind me taunted.

I tripped and stumbled, fell hard onto my hands and knees. He laughed and pounced on me. I fell down, lying on my belly as he covered his body with mine.

"You like that, don't you?"

I screamed and whimpered. The next thing I knew I was standing in the center of the hole. It was filling up with water, the rain falling at impressive speed. He stood above me, staring down as water poured over his face and chest. He wasn't wearing a shirt. As I stared, he tossed a rope ladder down to me, offering me freedom.

"Come up and play," he sang.

I jerked awake, sitting up in the center of the bed, the blankets twisted around my thighs. I searched the darkness of my room, assuring myself that I was alone and I was safe.

But I wasn't. Not really.

He was still out there. He could be doing the same thing to someone else. He could be looking for me.

What would happen if he found me?

I pushed the hair out of my face and got out of bed. No more sleeping. Not right now.

I went into the kitchen and pulled out a wooden cutting board, a knife, and a bag of green apples. I added a blue pie pan and all the ingredients I needed to make homemade piecrust. I always used my grandmother's recipe. I knew it by heart.

Just before I rolled out the dough, there was a muffled knock on the front door.

I froze and glanced at the clock. It was well after eleven p.m.

I grabbed the little knife off the counter and went to the top of the stairs where I stared at the door and wondered if I should answer.

24

Nathan

I hit the weights as soon as I got home. I literally parked the Jeep beside the house and jogged into the house in the fading light of day. I didn't bother to change. I just stripped off my shirt as I went down the steps into the unfinished basement.

It was cold down here, and the thud of my boots rang out over the concrete floor. My weight bench was set up in the center of the room. It was a welcome sight. I hadn't always enjoyed working out as much as I did now, but I found it was a good way to keep stress in check. It was a good way to blow off steam without getting drunk and spending half my life in some alcohol-induced stupor.

Besides, it seemed like a better idea to channel all my energy into something positive than drowning myself in a bottle.

Before I got started, I docked my iPhone on the speakers and cranked up some Aerosmith. I warmed up with a run on the treadmill. The pace started out casual but then worked up to a flat-out sprint. I liked the way my muscles exerted themselves. I was able to focus in on my body and my breath. Everything else fell away for a little while.

Once I was good and warm, I wiped my brow with the back of my arm and hit the weights. Usually I alternated muscle groups. Tonight I worked a little bit of everything. I went on autopilot doing bench presses, curls, and squats. After those were completed, I moved into push-ups and pull-ups. In the Corps, we were required to be able to do twenty pull-ups. I did forty.

I worked out for at least an hour, putting my body through its paces, and then I finished off by hanging from my pull-up bar upside down and holding a twenty pound disk to my chest while I did sit-ups.

When I was done, I stripped down naked and tossed all my clothes in the washing machine. As I walked upstairs, I checked my phone. And I wondered about Honor.

I took a quick shower and threw on a pair of dark-grey Nike sweatpants and a long-sleeved white T-shirt. Then I grabbed a beer out of the fridge and sat down in front of the flat-screen.

I turned on the news, hoping to see some breaking story about the arrest of Lex.

But I didn't see that.

"Local police are still searching for the man they believe responsible for the disappearance of Mary Alderson several weeks ago. They now believe the suspect, a Mr. Lex Sullman, is responsible for many of the kidnappings in the area over the last year. The police department issued an arrest warrant for Sullman early this morning when another young woman, who

*happens to be best-selling author Honor Calhoun, was brought
into the Allentown ER for treatment to several injuries that she
claims she received at the hands of Mr. Sullman. Ms. Calhoun
claims that Sullman abducted her early yesterday morning and
held her hostage near the town of Slatington. Ms. Calhoun's
injuries have been treated and sources tell us she has been
released from the hospital and is now resting at home.*

*"The search for Mr. Sullman continues. If you have any
information about this man, please contact your local police
department immediately."*

I stared at the pictures that flashed on the screen
as the anchor blabbed to all the damn world. When
she said Honor's name, my blood ran cold, and then
she flashed a picture of her, one that showed her face
completely unmarked.

I was right.

She was even more gorgeous without bruises.

Then a photo of Lex popped up on the screen.
He looked like a regular guy. He was someone that no
one would suspect of something like this.

He was still out there.

And if he was anywhere with a TV, he now knew
Honor's full name. And that meant her address
wouldn't be hard to find.

I got up from the couch, leaving the beer on the
coffee table. I grabbed my keys, another jacket, and
jammed my feet into a pair of sneakers. I left the TV
and the lights on and locked the door behind me.

When I got behind the wheel, I pulled my phone
out of my pocket. I could just call her. Ask her how
she was.

I shook my head and started the engine.

A phone call wasn't good enough.

I had to see, see with my own eyes that she was okay. And I sure as hell wasn't going to leave her alone the entire night while her kidnapper was pissed off and still out there.

I swore. Thanks to the f-ing news, not only was Lex pissed off, but now he was very well informed.

I called up her address in my memory and drove there in record time. Across the street from her house was a small pull-off shoulder on the road. I pulled off there and parked, checking out the surroundings, looking for anything that seemed out of place.

Her house was dark, and I wondered if it was because she wasn't home or if it was because she was asleep.

I settled back in the seat, thinking I was acting like a crazy stalker and how my mother would kick my ass if she saw me now. I didn't know what else to do. I couldn't just sit around at home and wonder if she was okay, not after watching the news.

Her house was pretty nice looking. Not real big, but still a decent size. It was newer looking with vinyl siding and white trim around the windows. The driveway was gravel and led to a two-car garage. A set of concrete steps led up to a covered front entryway and a large porch light hung just above. It was on, which made me think she might be home. The front door was painted yellow, a welcoming sunny color.

Off to the right of the house was a wooded area. The perfect place for some crazy ass to hide. I was pretty sure that behind her house ran the Slate Heritage trail. The trail ran for thirty miles and was built on an old railroad. It was also the trail she was attacked on. It would lead Lex right to her door.

I knew then that I would be spending the night. I would rather feel like a stalker than hear about her murder on the news in the morning.

Besides, I was a lot of things. A stalker wasn't one of them.

Outside, the wind beat against the ragtop of the Jeep, rattling the vinyl windows, but I didn't mind the sound. It helped keep me awake. I was tired. I was operating on a couple hours of sleep, and the thorough workout I did mellowed out my body.

A little while later, a light clicked on in one of the windows of Honor's house. I sat up a little straighter. Now I knew she was home. I watched the house, wondering what she was doing, waiting for the light to click off or another to click on. Neither happened.

The suspense of not knowing what was happening in there drove me insane. I debated for a while until I couldn't debate anymore.

I was knocking. I was just gonna have to admit that I was out here. She would probably be mad. She would probably tell me to leave and then bolt the door.

But at least I would know she was safe.

Mind made up, I jumped out of the Jeep and jogged across the street. She had potted flowers lining the concrete steps. I paused at the front door, listening for any kind of sound. There was none.

I lifted my hand and knocked.

Several minutes ticked by. I didn't knock again. I could almost feel her hovering on the other side of the wood. She was probably scared.

"Honor, it's Nathan," I yelled.

I heard a few locks unlatch and then the door opened a fraction, enough for one blue eye to peer out. Above her dark head was a sturdy-looking chain across the door. "Nathan?"

"Hey," I replied. "I know it's late. But I was worried—"

She slammed the door in my face.

I figured that meant she didn't want to see me. As I turned to walk away, I heard the chain on the door being slid free. I turned back.

The door opened.

Honor launched herself out of the house and into my arms.

"Hey," I said, catching her against me, trying not to squeeze her too hard around the chest. "What's the matter? Are you okay?"

She nodded against me but said nothing. Her feet were bare against the cold concrete of the porch. I lifted her up and went inside, pushing the door shut behind us. I took a moment to throw a couple of the locks before turning back to her. I chose not to acknowledge the knife clutched in her hand. But later we were going to have a talk about proper weapons.

She was wearing an oversized gray T-shirt and a pair of skintight black leggings. Her dark hair fell around her shoulders and cascaded down the center of her back. She still wore a bandage on her hand and some of the swelling around her eye had gone down.

"Are you okay?" I asked again.

"Yeah."

"What are you doing up? It's late?"

"I couldn't sleep." Her eyes met mine. I knew the look that swam in their depths.

I ran the pad of my finger over the dark smudge beneath her eye that wasn't swollen. "Bad dreams?"

She nodded again.

[169]

"You should have gone home with your mother," I said sternly.

"I'm making pie."

I couldn't really be mad about the change of subject. I mean, she was talking about pie. "You're making pie?"

"Apple. Wanna help?"

"Do cows have tails?"

She giggled and started up the steps that led into the living room and kitchen. I left my shoes down by the door and followed behind her.

I would have followed even if she didn't have pie.

25

Honor

The relief that flowed through my veins when Nathan called out from the other side of the door wasn't surprising. Considering the fact that I thought it was Lex, anyone would have made me weak with relief.

Except that isn't why I was relieved.

I *wanted* to see Nathan. Even through the silence of my thoughts, the taunting of the memories, and the nightmares of my dreams, there was one constant.

Him.

It was his image that I clung to when I finally fell asleep. And it was him that pulled me into the kitchen to bake a pie when I was feeling sort of lost.

And now he was here—standing in my kitchen, staring at me like I might up and disappear. I wanted to tell him I wouldn't go anywhere without him. But that was stupid. I was a grown woman. I was independent. I was holding a knife, dammit.

He didn't ask me why I was baking a pie. In fact, he seemed thrilled. It made me smile. This guy loved his pie. I looked at him, feeling my heart accelerate just a little as I remembered how close we'd come to kissing earlier.

What a sharp disappointment that had been. My lips practically ached to touch his. Looking at him now only made that ache deeper, made it reach all the way down into the deepest places inside me.

He was wearing a pair of dark-grey Nike sweatpants. They were a little big so they dipped incredibly low on his hips. The drawstring wasn't tied and the white ends trailed down, peeking from beneath the white shirt that clung to his body. I wondered what he would do if I grabbed hold of those strings, if I gave them a tug. Would he follow? Would he press me up against the counter and kiss me senseless?

He still hadn't shaved so the bottom half of his face was shadowed and prickly looking. He looked tired around his eyes and I wondered how much sleep he really got the night before.

Maybe I should've asked him what he was doing here in the middle of the night, but I didn't really care. I trusted him; I knew him. No, I guess I didn't know him, not in a traditional sense. I didn't know his favorite movie. I didn't know about his hobbies, his past, or his job.

But what I did know was far more important.

I knew the type of man he was.

I could spend years with a man and still never learn the kinds of things I already learned about Nathan. We'd already been through the kind of situation that showed what people were made of.

We'd already been through an event that totally bonded us.

The rest was just details.

As I mentioned before. I'm a writer. I'm a romantic. Go with it, people.

Nathan was the kind of guy who would literally stick his neck out for someone who needed help. He was the kind of man who wouldn't run from a dangerous situation. He barely flinched when I told the police what Lex had done to me, and while I could feel the anger that sometimes simmered just beneath his surface, I knew that he would never turn that anger on me.

I was safe with him.

"Nice place," he said, looking around my simple kitchen with the dark cabinets, dark-green countertops, and black appliances.

"Thanks." It wasn't a palace, but it was comfortable, and I was able to buy it off the money I made from my books. Never in a million years did I think my dream would afford me enough to live without having to work a day job. I owed it all to my readers.

That thought gave me a little pang of guilt. Those readers were probably wondering what happened to me.

"Honor?" Nathan asked, watching me closely.

I smiled and extended the knife toward him. "Wanna help?"

"I usually don't make pie. I just eat it," he said as he took the utensil.

"You eat, you cook."

He saluted me. "Aye-aye."

I showed him the apples. "You can peel these."

We worked silently side by side. I liked having him here. Even though he didn't say much, it wasn't so quiet anymore.

After I rolled out the crust and draped it in the pie pan, I added the sugar and smidge of flour to the sliced apples. Then I reached for the cinnamon and after I added a tablespoon, I went to set it down.

"It needs more." Nathan observed.

"You like cinnamon?" I asked, intrigued.

He nodded. I grinned. "Me too. I always add extra, but I wasn't sure if you'd like it or not."

"Add it in there, woman."

I added another generous heap.

"That's the stuff," he said.

After it was all tossed together, I poured it all in the crust and added the top layer, crimping the edges and cutting a few slits in the top. Nathan watched me carefully as I added an egg wash and sprinkled extra sugar over the top.

When it was done, he held open the oven door as I slid in the pie to bake.

"Want some coffee?" I asked.

Once we both had coffee with generous amounts of cinnamon creamer, I led him into the living room where I settled on the couch. He sat down beside me and I was glad he was close. That's one of the things I liked so much about Nathan. There was an unapologetic honesty about him. A "this is who I am" attitude. He didn't sit farther away from me because he was nervous or because he thought it would be more appropriate. He did what he wanted.

I was really hoping he wanted me.

"Wanna tell me about your dream?" he asked quietly.

I wrapped my hands around the mug, letting the warmth seep into me. I think one of the reasons I loved coffee so much was just because I liked holding the warm cup. "Not really."

He nodded and didn't press. "How's the ribs?"

"Peachy."

He chuckled. "When's my pie gonna be ready?"

"*Your* pie?" I asked and arched a brow.

"Do you often make apple pie in the middle of the night?"

"All the time." I scoffed.

He grinned. He knew I was lying.

"Will the dreams go away?" I whispered.

His smile slipped away. He sat forward and placed his mug on the coffee table and turned his body toward me. "I hope so."

"You have them too," I said, knowing his understanding went far beyond empathy.

"Sometimes."

I glanced at the scars on his face. Then I leaned my cheek against the cushions. "You should tell me about your problems. It'll make me feel better."

He chuckled. "Hearing about someone else's drama will make you feel better?"

"Yep."

I thought he might tell me to bug off.

"You really want to know?"

"I really do."

"I work as an armor man in the Marines. I'm in charge of inspecting the weapons, cleaning them, putting them together properly, stuff like that. A couple years ago, my unit deployed to Afghanistan. It's a rough country. A hellhole really. The Corps's presence over there was fairly new when I was sent.

There wasn't much in the way of comfort. We hadn't been there long enough to get things fully set up. We didn't have phones, the Internet was shoddy, and mostly we slept in tents."

I listened aptly, taking it all in, and the writer in me constructed a setting in my head that went along with his words.

"I'm not a grunt, meaning I don't fight on the front lines… but that doesn't mean there wasn't danger."

"I would think being there was danger enough. For anyone," I said.

He nodded. "For some more than others. It really just depends on the person's billet—their job."

I nodded and he continued. "One night the guys were short staffed and due out for patrol. It's basically routine—some guys go out and walk the perimeter of the base. They check certain areas, make sure our security is still tight. Make sure no enemy threat is lurking or lying in wait."

"Right," I agreed and took a sip of my coffee. The sound of his voice was incredible. I could listen to him talk for hours and not once get bored. There was a richness in his tone, a southern lilt that made his words a little more drawn out than most of the people that lived in this area.

"I volunteered to go with them, me and a couple other guys. We got some weapons and all of us headed out, small groups of us going in different directions."

He got this faraway look in his eyes, and I knew he was going back there, that whatever scene he was reliving replayed vividly in his mind. I scooted a little closer, something pushing me forward, like I instinctively knew he was going to need the comfort.

"It was pretty typical at first, us just patrolling, making sure everything was fine. And it was. Until we were attacked."

His voice took on a more gravelly tone. "I was out with two other guys, good guys. Young guys. They had their entire lives ahead of them. One of them just had a baby. All he could talk about was getting home to meet his baby girl."

Please, God, tell me he made it home.

"We were on the far side of the base, near the weaponry tent. We didn't keep too much else around the weapons. It was just a safety precaution. There were a few tents here and there, as was the tent I spent a lot of my time in, readying weapons. It was night, so there weren't many men around. Most were at chow or already bunked down for the night.

"Everything seemed fine and we were about to head back toward the other side of base when I caught a slight sound. The sound of a weapon being cocked. I knew that sound. I knew it better than most. I heard it hundreds of times a day. It was my job to know that sound.

"I pivoted toward the sound, only it wasn't coming from within the base—it was coming from outside our boundaries."

A look of sheer despair crossed his face, and I reached out, wrapping my hand around his. He looked down to where my hand touched his. Without saying anything, he threaded our fingers together and gave mine a gentle squeeze.

Then his brows knit together when he took in the bruise and rash across the top of my hand. He lifted my arm and pressed a soft kiss to the irritated area. "IV?" he asked once his lips left my skin.

I nodded. "I have sensitive skin. That tape was brutal."

"I should have watched the nurse."

"You did more than enough for me," I told him.

His thumb began to make slow circles across the back of my hand, and his eyes began to slip away once more. "I called a warning as enemy fire started peppering the sand around our feet. We all dropped to the ground and returned fire, but it was so dark out there it was hard to know where to aim. I listened for the popping of gunfire and aimed in the direction of the sound."

"If this is too hard," I told him gently, not wanting to hurt him further by making him speak.

He shook his head. I think he wanted to get it out there.

"There were more of them than there were of us. It became evident that they wanted to raid the weapons tent. They wanted to take all of our supplies and use them against us."

I said a dirty cuss word. He smiled.

"Gidding radioed for backup, and I knew the men close by were able to hear the gunfire. It wouldn't be long until we had numbers and weapons on our side. Unfortunately, the enemy seemed to know that too. They launched some sort of grenade right as, blowing up a couple tents and taking out one of the guys. It was Gidding. He was my friend."

He looked at me. "Sometimes at night, I can still hear him screaming."

I scooted a little bit closer. He pulled up his left knee and dropped his right foot onto the floor. I settled myself in the small opening between his legs.

"One of the hostile's made a run for the main weapon tent. Me and Prior went after him. Prior was the one with the new baby. As we ran, a couple of them appeared out of nowhere, aiming their weapons and letting go a couple rounds. Prior took a hit in the shoulder and the thigh. One of the bullets bounced off the ground and hit me in the calf."

He lifted up the sweats around his left leg and showed me a knotted white scar.

"I let loose with all the ammo in my gun and took the fuckers out. Prior tried to keep going, but one of the bullets hit an artery in his leg. The blood… it was like a freaking fountain the way it spurted from his leg. I picked him up and carried him toward the tent, where I figured we would at least be shielded from more gunfire."

The image in my head of Nathan bleeding and limping while gunfire and screaming erupted around him made my heart hurt. I pictured the way he must have looked dressed in boots and cammies, carrying an empty gun and his friend who was clinging to life.

"We made it to the weapons tent. I laid him out on the ground and tied my blouse around his leg as tight as I could. I screamed my head off for a medic and sent one of the guys who was running into the fray back out of it to hunt down the Corpsman."

Nathan looked up at me.

"He didn't want to die. He had everything to live for."

"Of course not," I said sympathetically. I knew then that Nathan's friend Prior didn't make it. I knew that out there somewhere was a little girl without a father and a woman with a broken life.

"I told him I'd get him out of there," Nathan said, his voice breaking on his words.

"What happened?"

"I grabbed a new gun and started fighting, holding them back from the tent. Our guys got a leg up, the hostile's were waning, and I knew they would be out of ammo soon. When the medic came into site, I grabbed another gun and ran out into the open. The fire started coming my way and I hoped it would create enough of a distraction for them to get to Prior."

He glanced up at me. "He died, Honor."

"That's not your fault," I promised him.

"They were pissed they weren't going to be getting our weapons... so they launched a grenade at the tent. I saw it falling through the sky. I knew what was going to happen. I yelled. I ran toward them all. I wanted to get Prior and the medics out of there. But I was too late. The entire tent blew in a massive blast. All that ammo..." he said, his voice trailing away.

"You ran toward the tent?" I asked incredulously. "Even after you saw the grenade?"

He looked at me. "Yes. I was the reason they were in there. Prior was lying in there because I told him he'd be safe."

"You couldn't have known they would blow the place up."

"I should have thought that far ahead. I should have been in there to get him out."

I reached up and touched the jagged scar across his cheek. The scar he got while trying to save other men's lives. He could've ran away. He could have ducked and covered.

He didn't.

He almost died trying to save them.

"I'm so glad you didn't die," I whispered.

He stilled and looked me in the eyes. "I should have died with them. They died for my mistake. The blast was so strong it threw me backward. That's what saved my life."

I sat up just a little bit straighter and took his face in the palms of my hands. He watched me through somber blue eyes as I leaned forward and pressed a kiss to the reminder of the night he almost died. The scar was puckered and raised a bit, so I kissed it again. When I pulled away, I ran my thumb over the scar just below his bottom lip.

Before I could stop myself, I leaned forward and gently kissed the underside of that lip, aiming directly for the scar.

He made a soft sound and brought his hands up to cup my face.

The oven timer chose that moment to beep.

He didn't let go; he didn't move a muscle.

"Your pie's ready," I whispered.

He helped me off the couch and I pulled the nicely browned and bubbly pie out of the oven and set it aside to cool. When I turned to race back into the living room, I bumped into his solid chest.

I hadn't realized he followed.

He slipped his hands beneath my arms and lifted me onto the counter, stepping between my legs. Without a second thought, I wrapped them around his waist, pulling him just a little bit closer.

His hand delved into my hair and his mouth descended upon mine.

The scent of apples and cinnamon mixed with his heady pine scent and my eyes slid shut as his lips moved over mine. He kissed like he did everything else, with honesty and no holding back.

His lips were thick and full, insistent and soft. Every inch of my mouth surrendered to him as we met again and again and again. Nathan moved one hand around the base of my neck and used his thumb to tilt my chin up a little bit more, granting himself more access as his tongue slipped inside and began exploring my mouth.

I grabbed ahold of his biceps and hung on, squeezing his muscles and answering his kiss. I used my tongue to stroke his and lick across his luscious bottom lip and sucked it into my mouth and teased it with my teeth. He groaned and slid me across the counter until I wasn't really sitting on it anymore, but I was being held against him by his strong arms.

My center was pressed against his rock-hard abs, and I felt the center of me begin to throb like my heartbeat was suddenly coming from down there. Moisture slicked my panties and he kissed me even deeper. I locked my ankles together behind his back and he groaned, stepping away from the counter completely and carrying me out into the living room.

He didn't lay me out on the couch like I thought he would. Instead, he sat down and kept me in his lap. The change in position brought me up against the solid erection beneath the fabric of his sweats, and without thinking, I rocked against it.

A shudder moved through him and he pulled away and reclined against the cushions.

I was breathing heavy when he spoke.

"We should slow down."

No. No we shouldn't. I'd never felt like this, um, *ever*, and he wanted me to give it up?

"This isn't why I came over here."

"Why did you?" I asked, my voice still entirely breathless.

He swiped at my lower lip, frowning at the area that was still slightly swollen. "Because I wanted to be sure you were okay. I hadn't planned on knocking, but I saw your light come on."

"You understand," I said.

He nodded slowly. "Some. I understand what's it like to be in a situation you feel you have no control over. I know what it's like to fight for your life even when death is trying to claim you."

"You also know what it's like to feel guilty you survived when someone else did not."

He sat up abruptly, our chests bumped together, and he splayed a hand across my upper back. "I don't want you feeling guilty, Honor."

I lowered my eyes. "I do. We both know Mary is dead."

"He's going to pay for what he did to her. To you."

I leaned against his chest. He was so big that I fit against him with no problem. I tucked my hands between us and rested my head against his shoulder, curling in as close as I could. "Why don't you try and get some sleep?" he murmured, stroking the back of my head.

"M'kay." I agreed, snuggling even closer.

He chuckled. "As much as I like you where you are, if you stay like that, your ribs are going to hate you in the morning."

"Don't care," I mumbled.

His chest rumbled with his quiet laugh and I felt his lips graze the top of my head. "Up you go," he said, standing up and bringing me with him.

I groaned.

"Where's your room?"

"Last door on the right," I directed when he turned down the hall.

The bathroom light was still on, providing a soft light illuminating the bedroom. Holding me with one arm, he threw back the covers with another and deposited me in the center of the bed. Nathan tucked the covers up around me as I sank into the pillows.

"Are you leaving?" I asked, wanting him to stay.

"I'll take the couch."

"Really?"

"Unless you want me to go."

I lifted up the covers, inviting him in. "I want you to stay."

He stood there looking down for long moments. "Fine. But no funny business," he said as he stripped off his shirt. "I got a reputation to protect."

It was the perfect opening for a smart-ass comeback. Too bad I was too busy staring at his incredibly chiseled chest to make one. I was pretty sure he didn't have an ounce of fat on him. His dog tags hung between his sculpted pecs, giving them even more definition. And he had a tattoo—the letters USMC spelled vertically down the side of his well-defined abs.

I was almost sorry when he slid between the sheets because I couldn't look at him any longer.

I said almost.

The feel of him against me was even better than the picture he made standing beside me. I threw an arm across his waist, my fingers flirting with the waistband of his pants.

"I'm only staying because you're feeding me pie for breakfast," he said a moment later.

I smiled into the darkness. "And here I thought you never lied," I said.

He laughed. "Technically, it's not a lie if you already know the truth."

"What's the truth, Nathan?" I whispered, tucking myself closer to his side.

"There's nowhere else I'd rather be."

No more nightmares bothered me that night.

26

Nathan

Sunlight filtered through the drawn shades in the room, casting a golden glow over the entire space. Honor was lying right next to me, her entire body pressed up against mine. It was the first time I'd ever slept in a bed with a woman the entire night.

Usually, when I was in a woman's bed, it wasn't for sleeping, but for sex. And yeah, I wanted to have sex with Honor so badly I could barely think straight. If she was anybody else, I would have had her naked in less than two hours.

But she wasn't like anyone else.

I turned and took in her sleeping face. Her head was turned toward me and dark chestnut-colored hair was spread out across her pillow, one long strand falling over her eye. One of her hands was tucked between my arm and my side and the feeling of her fingers curled against my bare skin sent another wave of longing through me.

I needed a cold shower. But I wasn't about to get out of this bed. I guess I was going to have to take my torture like a man this morning. Hell, I was going to like it.

Her skin was unlined and smooth, with cheekbones that were high and broad, creating a heart shape out of her face. Her lips were a pale peach color and were just slightly parted in her sleep. From this angle, it appeared the swelling around the bottom was gone.

Kissing her last night had been fucking awesome.

It took everything in me to restrain myself, but I knew I had to go slow. We'd only known each other for a short time and the circumstances of our meeting had not been… traditional. Some man had just abused her and I wasn't going to push her any further than she wanted to go.

In sleep, she sighed contentedly, and I brushed the wayward strand of hair away from her face. A guy like me could get used to a girl like her.

Her eyes blinked awake and the blue orbs focused on me, her lips curling into a smile.

"Hey," I said, brushing at her hair again.

"Hi."

Was that a hint of shyness in her tone? I turned onto my side and slid down so we were face to face. Then I went in for a kiss.

"Wait!" she gasped, burying her face into the pillow.

"You didn't complain last night," I muttered.

Her giggle was muffled against the pillow. Then she said, "Mooony brooothhe."

"What?" I laughed, trying to make out her words.

She lifted her face. "Morning breath!"

I grunted. "I got it too. Now come over here and give me a smelly kiss."

"No!"

I arched an eyebrow, but she wasn't looking at me. She was still hiding in the pillow. As gently as I could, I hauled her up across my chest and grasped her face between my palms. "Kiss me."

I didn't wait for her to obey. I went and got what I wanted. At first she tried to kiss me timidly, barely opening her mouth, almost giving me a chaste little kiss. Yeah, that wasn't cutting it for me. So I kissed her one way and then changed direction and went the other. Using the tip of my tongue, I licked across the center of her lips and she moaned, giving me the perfect opportunity to slip inside.

After that, she forgot about her supposed morning breath and kissed me with a reckless abandon that actually made me forget to breathe. I was a guy. I was supposed to be in control of the situation. But Honor had taken over the driver's seat and was leading me around with every single stroke of her hot little tongue.

Her hands began to explore my chest and her feather-light touch drove me wild. I couldn't help the way my hips thrust up off the mattress against her, and I froze when my erection brushed up against her belly. I didn't want to scare her.

She didn't act upset. In fact, she liked it. Her hips automatically drove forward to meet mine.

My eyes shot open.

Yeah, I was a strong guy, but I wasn't a freaking saint.

I gave her one last lingering kiss and then pulled back and looked up into her face. Her cheeks were flushed and the swelling around her eye was almost completely gone.

I lifted my head and pressed a kiss to the corner where it was most bruised. "How ya feeling?"

She grimaced. "Sore."

"It's always worse the next day."

She laid her head against my chest and groaned. Then she stilled. "What's the matter?"

"You're not wearing a shirt."

"I'm offended you just noticed."

"Oh, I didn't just notice," she purred. Her lips began pressing kisses up the center toward my neck.

I swear she left a trail of flames in her wake. I groaned. Heat licked up my thighs and my rock-solid length jerked in response. I don't think I'd ever been so hard. It was almost painful. All I could think about was driving myself deep inside her until all the lust within me was spent.

When her teeth closed around my earlobe, I pulled her away. "You have no idea what you're doing to me," I ground out.

She smiled a lazy, sleepy smile. "I think I might have an idea."

I swatted her bottom. "Get off me, woman."

She titled her head and squinted at me. "You sure you're not gay?"

I snatched up her hand and pressed it to the evidence of me *not* being gay. "Unless you're secretly a really hot dude, then no, I'm not gay."

Her eyes widened a bit and then her mouth fell open in a little O. "That's, umm," she said and cleared her throat. Then she giggled. "That's some pretty large evidence."

"Damn straight," I said arrogantly.

"You sure you don't want to stay in bed?"

I couldn't believe the words that were about to come out my mouth. "Yes. I'm sure."

She made a harrumphing sound and rolled over. I got out of bed before I dove myself at her and did what I told myself I wasn't going to do.

I looked down as I stood. The tent in my pants wasn't something I could hide. Damn. I was going to be frustrated all damn day now. I went into the bathroom and splashed some ice-cold water on my face, rinsed out my mouth, and used the facilities.

It was chilly this morning so when I came out of the bathroom, I snatched up my shirt and yanked it on. Honor was still in bed.

"My entire body feels like a giant bruise." She moaned.

"Up you go," I said and lifted her off the mattress and held her in my arms. On my way to the door, she pointed to a pair of fuzzy looking boots.

"I need my slippers."

I bent and she grabbed them, and then I carried her out into the kitchen where I deposited her on a chair at the table. "I'll make you some coffee."

She put on her slippers as she told me where she kept the coffee, and I got a pot brewing. The apple pie on the counter called out to me, and my stomach grumbled. As the coffee brewed, I spied the bottle of pain meds the doctor gave her at the hospital, and I set them in front of her along with a glass of water.

"Those will help with the soreness."

Dutifully, she swallowed her pill and then I poured her a cup of coffee and handed it to her with the creamer.

"You're a pretty handy guy to have around," she said, stirring her coffee and creamer together.

"I know."

She laughed and it made me turn my head to look at her. She looked tiny sitting there at the table with her hair all a mess and a steaming mug cradled between her hands. Even with bruises on her face, she was beautiful to me. Without thinking, I strode across the room and swooped in to plant a lingering kiss on her cinnamon-flavored lips.

When I pulled back, her eyes looked a little dazed, and I mentally patted myself on the back. *Good job, Nathan.*

"You have any ice cream?" I asked, snooping through her freezer.

"No."

"You know that's like a crime. Pie with no ice cream."

"I'm sorry?" she asked.

I sighed heavily. "I'm still eating pie."

"I'd tell you to make yourself at home, but you already have," she quipped.

I grinned and rummaged for a bowl and a knife. I did feel at home here, from the second I stepped through the front door. I felt like I was where I belonged, like this wasn't my first night here. It felt perfectly natural for me to be making coffee and kissing her good morning. This was what I wanted. Not just today. Not just next week...

"Nathan?" Honor said from across the room.

I glanced over. She was giving me a puzzled look. "Where'd you go?"

My thoughts had stilled my movements and I was standing in the center of the room, clutching a knife and a bowl. "Nowhere." I lied and cut a huge piece of pie. I wondered what she would say if I told her I was already thinking about forever.

"You're putting pie into a bowl?"

"There's no ice cream," I explained.

"Yes, I realize the error of my ways." I heard the smile in her voice.

I reached into the fridge, pulled out the milk, and poured some into the bowl, over the pie. "A man's gotta do what a man's gotta do," I told her and heated up the bowl in the microwave.

"Apple pie. It's what's for breakfast," Honor said, as I sat down beside her.

"It's got milk. It's like cereal."

She shook her head and drank more coffee.

The first bite exploded onto my tongue. "Oh my God." I groaned. "This is the best thing I've ever eaten."

She laughed.

"No really," I said as I shoved another bite into my mouth. "You are a pie genius."

Honor rolled her eyes. I scooped out another bite and held it to her lips. "Try it." Her lips parted and I slid the spoon over her tongue and then pulled it back out, watching the way her lips hugged the silver. My body tightened all over again.

"It's good." She agreed.

Pie this good deserved some silence, so I didn't say anything as I shoveled the rest into my mouth.

"Usually by now I would be on my way home from my morning run," she murmured, looking out the sliding glass doors near the table and at the trail.

"You run every day of the week?"

"Most mornings. Not every day."

I wondered if she would keep running out there after what happened to her.

"How about you? You must work out a lot."

"Almost every day."

"Do you like being a Marine?" she asked.

"It's okay. I think about getting out sometimes. Living somewhere that I won't have to move from."

"Where are you from?"

"I grew up in Jacksonville, NC. It's a Marine Corps kind of town. I grew up sort of idolizing the Marines. I joined right out of high school and went to Paris Island for boot camp."

She smiled. "I knew I heard the South in your voice. Is this the first time you've lived up North?"

"Yep. It's cold."

She grinned. "How long you been enlisted?"

"Six years."

She nodded and put her mug to her lips. I took advantage and asked a question of my own. "Did you grow up here?"

She nodded. "Yes, never lived anywhere else."

"You said you're a writer?"

She looked a little shy as she nodded.

"What do you write?"

"Books."

"What kind of books?" Geez, it was like pulling teeth.

"Mostly romance novels. I also have some paranormal stuff."

"You mean like vampires?"

"Werewolves," she replied.

"You seem embarrassed," I pointed out, glancing over at the pie and thinking about getting another piece.

She laughed and stood up. "I'm not really. Just sometimes people's reaction to my career can be a little... harsh."

I watched as she moved stiffly over to the counter, taking my bowl with her, and cut another huge slice of pie.

"What do you mean?"

"Well, it's hard to get someone to take you seriously when you tell them you write romance or about werewolves."

I guess I could understand that. It was a little out there. Of course, me going to work and dealing with guns all day wasn't all that normal either.

"How long you been a writer?"

"I've always wanted to be a writer," she replied. "I've been writing stuff since I was young. But I started writing professionally about two and a half years ago. I had a day job up until about six months ago. Now, I'm able to write full time."

"You love it." I could tell by the look on her face.

She smiled and reached into the beeping microwave to get my pie. "Yeah, I really do."

When she sat the pie on front of me, I pulled her into my lap and rested my chin on top of her head. "You gonna give me one of your books to read?"

"You want to read my books?"

"I want to do anything that has anything to do with you."

"I'm glad you came over last night," she said, pressing her cheek against my chest.

"Me too."

We sat there for a while in the quiet of the kitchen, and for once, the silence didn't bother me at all.

27

Honor

Nathan was standing in front of the large glass sliders when I came out of the hallway and into the kitchen. He had his arms crossed over his chest and the position showed off his powerful back perfectly.

I swear, he was the stuff I wrote about.

I didn't think men like him actually existed outside of my imagination. And now he was living, breathing, and standing in front of me. *He slept in my bed last night.* Joyous little goose bumps raced over my entire body.

The sun shone through the glass, bathing him in this sort of halo so everything else around him was slightly blurred. It was the perfect representation of what he did to me. When he was around, everything else was hazy, but he was perfectly in focus.

The very fact that I was standing here secretly checking him out instead of dwelling on what I just went through was very telling.

Yes, it told me I was way too horny (hey, I write romance).

But… It also told me that what I was feeling for him was bigger than what happened to me. He completely eclipsed the fact that I was kidnapped and trapped. Yeah, I was still disturbed by what happened to me; however, it was impossible to dwell because of all the possibilities standing within my reach.

"You're lurking." he said without turning around.

"I do not lurk." I sniffed and moved farther into the room.

He chuckled and turned slightly so he could glance at me. His eyes roamed over my body, and I bit my lip in response to the delicious desire that surged over me. "The bath make you feel better?"

After we both consumed considerable amounts of coffee and pie, Nathan insisted I take a warm bath to help ease the soreness in my body. It wasn't hard to agree. A bath definitely was easier than a shower. I was able to let my hand with the stitches hang over the side.

"Between the coffee, the hot water, and the pain meds, I would say I'm good as new."

His eyes narrowed slightly.

"Okay, almost as good as new."

"Come here," he said softly, his voice like a rumble through the room.

I walked across the room, my furry boots shuffling over the tile floor. "Those boots are damned cute," he murmured, reaching out and drawing me in so we were standing face to face in front of the window.

"They're very warm."

He grasped my face and tilted it up and toward the light and studied me like I was some priceless piece of art. "Your eye looks a lot better."

"I can see out of it now and that's always a plus."

He frowned. I hadn't wanted to make him frown. To make it up to him, I leaned up all the way on my tiptoes and pressed my lips to his. He bent down slightly and wrapped both arms around my waist, pulling me closer.

I felt a little protest in my ribs, but I wasn't about to complain. His lips were the ultimate pain reliever.

He teased my lips, flirted with them. His kisses were short and raspy. Then they would change into long and seductive. Just as I would get used to one kiss and begin spiraling into deep desire, he would change his angle, his intensity, or the pressure of his mouth, and it would be an entirely new experience all over again.

He left all my senses reeling.

And that was only with his kiss.

I couldn't help but ask myself what he would be like in bed. Naked.

He pulled back and gentled his hold, dropping a quick kiss to my temple. "You smell like cinnamon."

"You still smell like a Christmas tree."

"Cinnamon and Christmas go together."

"Yeah," I murmured. "Yeah, they do." I dragged my hand along the back of his neck, caressing the smooth skin and then slipping my fingers beneath the neckline of his T-shirt.

He made a sound of appreciation, and I smiled.

"What do you have going on today?" he asked.

I wished I could say nothing. I wished I could sit in his arms every second of this day. "I promised my parents I would come over for a while. They're still pretty freaked out. And I have to get a new cell phone. It feels weird not having one. Plus, I really need it for work. I use it all the time."

"Are you a social media junkie?" He teased.

"It's my job." I defended my serious bad habit. "It's called marketing."

"Be careful today," he whispered against my lips and kissed me softly. My heart turned over. How such a big, rough guy could be so tender I would never understand.

"I don't think my social media obsession is dangerous." I joked.

"I'm not talking about your unhealthy online habits, sweetheart."

I couldn't even complain that he called my habits unhealthy because he went and added sweetheart at the end of his sentence. *sigh*

After my initial melty reaction, his true meaning broke through, and my stomach tightened. I knew what he was talking about. I just didn't want to think about it.

'Course, pushing it away wouldn't make the problem disappear; it would only make it worse. If I wanted all the potential that I felt Nathan presented, then I needed to deal with the here and now so I could realize those possibilities. "Yeah, I know," I said and pulled away to stare out the window at the trail. A woman was running along with a dog on a leash.

I watched them go, my eyes staying with the dog, a chocolate lab. I wondered what kind of dog I should get…

"Did you watch the news at all last night?"

"No," I answered as the dog and woman ran out of sight. I looked up at Nathan. "Why?"

"It's the reason I drove over here." He paused. "Well, one of the reasons."

"Tell me." I was going to face this head on and kick it in the balls.

"The media reported your name. Your full name. And they reported his name too. They connected him to Mary."

I felt the blood drain from my head. "Why would they do that?" I asked, dazed.

"Because the media is a bunch of bloodsucking drama hags."

I laughed. "I'm so going to use that in one of my books."

He grinned.

"So now he knows my name. And can find my address."

"Yeah, pretty much. Not only that, but we blew the whistle on his identity. He's a walking target."

"Maybe that will send him away. He will run to some place people won't know him."

Nathan considered my words. "It's definitely a possibility."

"But you don't think that's what he'll do."

He scrubbed a hand down his face. "Shit, Honor. I don't know. Part of me hopes to hell he runs to Mexico."

"And the other part?"

His eyes met mine. "The other part of me thinks we pissed him off. Badly. I'm afraid you've become a challenge to him, one he won't want to walk away from."

I shivered. His words were scary.

"I don't want to go back in that hole," I whispered. Everything inside me felt numb, like my body was locking down some sort of self-protection mechanism in preparation for something terrible.

He swore in a way that only a Marine could. "You're not going back in that hole," Nathan vowed and pulled me into his chest. I wrapped my arms around his middle and held tight, like he was the last rooted tree in a raging tornado.

"Wait here," he said and pulled away. I watched him go to the front door, unlock it, and walk out in the biting autumn wind.

A few minutes later, he came back inside. "I have something for you."

His hands were empty. "What is it?"

He came up the stairs and I met him at the top. He reached behind him and pulled something out of the back of his sweats.

It was a gun.

"I want you to take this."

I stared at it like it was the plague. "I don't want that."

"Yeah, I know. Take it anyway."

Given my situation, having a gun would be smart. I may not want to carry it around, but I knew to the bottom of my slipper boots that if Lex showed up I wouldn't hesitate to shoot him.

I'd probably shoot him more than once.

I took the gun, the weight of it not entirely foreign considering I carried one just like this the other night in the woods.

"You remember what I told you?" Nathan asked.

"Point and pull the trigger?"

"Yes." He showed me how to work the safety and then made me show him that I understood how to use it.

"Listen to me," he said once I knew exactly how to use the gun. "Shoot first. Ask questions later."

"Okay." Then I tucked the gun in my purse.

Nathan rolled his eyes.

"What?" I said. "Should I carry it in the back of my pants like you do?"

"Hell, no. You'd probably shoot yourself in that luscious ass."

I had to admit, I liked he thought my ass was luscious.

"You gonna be okay today?" he asked.

"Of course."

"Maybe you should just stay at your parents' house tonight," he suggested.

"I like my house."

"What about my house?" he asked.

"Your house?"

"You might like it there too. I have a king-sized bed." He arched an eyebrow at me and gave me "the look."

"What are you suggesting?" I asked. Inside, my nerves were fluttering around like a moth near a lamp.

"Stay with me tonight. It will be safer."

"Is that the only reason you want me to stay?"

He shook his head slowly. "I have this image," he began, reaching out to twirl a strand of my hair around two of his fingers, "of your hair spread out over my pillow and my sheets smelling like cinnamon."

"I should probably stay with you, then," I said, my lips curving into a smile. "For safety reasons, of course."

"Of course," he murmured as he stepped closer and claimed my lips in a gentle kiss.

I felt my nipples harden and crush against the silky fabric of my bra. I pressed myself closer to him, arching just a little, and his giant, warm palm settled over one of my breasts. I sighed and his tongue licked into my mouth as his hand gently squeezed my sensitive flesh. My bra and sweater annoyed me. They were in the way of what I knew would be an all-encompassing feeling.

I pushed my hand beneath the hem of his T-shirt and raked my nails up his abdomen, around to his lower back. Gripping his taut skin, I urged him closer.

One of his thighs slipped between my legs as he brought me fully up against him. My inner muscles clenched and the rapidly swelling and sensitive bud between my legs began to ache. I bore down against his solid thigh, looking for sweet release.

Everything inside me felt wound tight as tension continued to build. I made a small, desperate sound in the back of my throat and sank my nails into his back just a little bit more. My hips gyrated over his leg as he cupped my butt and pushed me more firmly against him.

"What do you want, sweetheart?" he murmured against my mouth.

I made another little sound, not really hearing his words. My body had taken over and it wasn't going to let me have control back until it got what it wanted.

His fingers moved to the button on my skinny jeans. The closure gave way to his nimble fingers and soon the zipper was gliding down. I shivered in anticipation. I'd never wanted anyone's hands on me this badly.

Nathan dipped his hand into the open waistband of the jeans and reached down to cup my throbbing vagina. I groaned because just the pressure of his hand brought me a little bit closer to the edge.

His tongue circled mine as he began to back us up, moving into the living room where he gently placed me on the edge of the coffee table. My feet were planted on the floor when I looked up at him, wondering what he was doing.

He kneeled before me, sliding my fuzzy boots off and tossing them over his shoulder. Then he hooked his fingers in the ankles of my jeans and pulled. I lifted my butt off the tabletop so he could tug them away.

Nathan sat back and looked at me for long moments. The skin on his palms was slightly rough as they slid up my legs and into the insides of my thighs. The white silk panties I wore were already damp with desire.

"Will you let me pleasure you, Honor?" Nathan asked, teasing the edge of my panties with his fingers.

"Yes," I answered, breathless, leaning all my weight into my hand without the stitches.

"You can say no right now," he said, pulling his hands away.

"I'm saying yes," I demanded, wanting his touch back.

He chuckled. It was a short-lived sound because he hooked both hands behind my knees and pulled me across the top of the table until my butt almost slid completely off. I watched with heavy lidded concentration as he planted my legs onto the carpet on either side of him and then he positioned himself at my center. Both his hands hooked into the waistband of the panties. "Up," he said gently and then he pulled them away, leaving me completely bare below the waist.

Nathan stroked the area where soft, short curls grew. My head fell back and my eyes slid closed as his fingers dipped into my very wet, deepest place. He didn't delve right in like I thought he might. Instead, he swirled his fingers around in the moisture, coating the entire area with my personal lubricant.

"It's like liquid satin," he said to himself as if he were utterly fascinated.

The more he circled his fingers around, the shorter my breaths became. He pinched and teased my folds until they felt thick and full. I was so very wet that some of the moisture coated the insides of my thighs.

The sensations rolling through me were just the tip of the iceberg. Nathan had just begun.

Very carefully he draped my legs over his shoulders so my knees bent and my calves fell down his back. He pressed a trail of kisses up the inside of my thigh and then he pulled one of my folds into his mouth and began to suck.

I jerked up off the table, the sparks of heat so intense that I thought I might burst into flames. He took his time with each and every part of me. There was no place neglected. By the time he made it to my center, I was shaking with need. I couldn't control it. It's like my body didn't know how to be still; there was just too much passion running rampant beneath my skin.

"Please, Nathan," I said, wanting to reach out for him but needing my elbows for support.

His tongue delved into my opening and I cried out, completely not expecting that he would use his tongue that way. It was so intimate that it was partially overwhelming. In and out his tongue moved, creating the same kind of action his hips would make if he were between my legs. He didn't delve too deeply inside me, but it was just enough.

His lips pulled at my clitoris and rolled around, massaging it.

I gasped and arched upward.

In one final act of freaking epic proportions, Nathan gripped my hips and towed me even farther forward. My backside was no longer touching the coffee table. He was completely supporting my weight and his face was totally immersed... well... you know where.

My entire world splintered apart. I shattered like a too-hot light bulb. Pieces of me flew everywhere, scattering around us. I couldn't think; all I could do was let the feeling of the orgasm ripple through my depths as my stomach muscles clenched over and over again.

He didn't stop licking, but his tongue gentled, bringing me back to Earth in the best way possible.

I collapsed against the hardwood surface of the table. Sweat actually beaded on my forehead and my legs still trembled.

Oh. My. God.

I should've probably been embarrassed. Yeah. No. I wasn't going to be embarrassed about that. It was mind blowing.

"I'm never going to look at this coffee table the same way again," I said as Nathan pulled back just slightly. He slid me a little farther onto the table but still supported my legs with his shoulders.

"You've got to be the hottest woman I have ever met."

I pushed up onto one elbow and shoved at the hair falling into my eyes. "You're not so bad yourself."

He looked smug. His lips were slightly swollen and his cheeks were flushed. I glanced down at the tent he was sporting in his pants.

"Looks like you could use some attention," I purred.

He grabbed my panties off the floor and slid them around my ankles. "It's not about me right now."

"Then what's it about?"

"You," he whispered, gliding the silk back up my legs. "Only you."

I sat up, swaying a little with the movement. I felt drunk. I felt woozy. I was completely and totally relaxed.

He smirked. "Besides. You've had all you can handle of me right now."

"You don't think I can handle you?" I said, stubbornness crawling into my tone.

Nathan scooted forward on both his knees, wrapping an arm around my waist and using his free hand to tuck the hair behind my ear. "I know you can. I'm actually a little worried I won't be able to handle you."

Something inside me softened. I laid a hand on his cheek. "I'm not gonna hurt you, Nathan Reed."

He smiled a little sadly. The longing in his eyes pulled at my heart.

"I know you wouldn't. Not intentionally. But not all hurt can be prevented."

What did he mean by that?

28

Nathan

Life is fragile. A man knows this from the time he's just a boy, but for me, it didn't really sink in until I watched men die around me.

Before I went to Afghanistan, I was young. There was a freedom I always felt, like life was limitless and so was time. I didn't really think about how we could be here one moment and gone the next.

And then I went to war.

I watched men—*good men*—die. I watched the fear in their eyes as hostile people shot and attacked us. I heard the yelling, the screaming. Desperation and gunfire laced the air and sounds of the explosion still haunted my every waking hour.

When I returned home, I wasn't the young man who left. I felt old. I felt hardened, and I glanced at men who I used to be like and felt angry they could be so innocent I wanted to rage at them; I wanted to tell them they had no idea the time they wasted.

I wanted to tell them that everyone has an expiration date and they needed to start living like it.

But I didn't.

I couldn't give out advice I wasn't living. *Lead by example.* It was something I tried to lay as the foundation of my career in the Marine Corps. To me, that meant being a Marine, a man that my peers could look up to. It meant showing others how to live with actions.

But my actions went against everything I learned in Afghanistan.

Instead of living life to the fullest and making the most of every minute, I sort of withdrew. I shied away from things I really enjoyed, from the people I really loved, because living life to the fullest felt too hard.

Living life to the fullest was dangerous.

It was easier to avoid commitment, avoid attachments, and be solitary because part of me thought it would hurt less. Some of those men were like brothers to me. Their lives ended in the blink of an eye.

I went and stood at their funerals and watched their loved ones cry. I watched Prior's wife cry over his gravesite while she cradled the baby daughter he never got to meet.

How was that fair?

How was it fair that he died and I got to live?

What made my life more valuable than his?

And so I retreated. I spent my days working out and filling my time.

I didn't want to live that way anymore.

Honor was the light that flooded my darkness. She was the glasses to my partially blind eyes. Her kisses were like balm to my wounded soul. Her determination to survive even when odds were against her was my wakeup call.

I told her I was afraid I wouldn't be able to handle her. I didn't mean sexually. I had that shit handled. That woman turned to putty in my hands. I meant emotionally. Honor was the kind of woman that would make me fall. It would be hard and fast, and once I was in love with her, I knew I would love her forever.

What if she died too?

What if I gave her everything I had and then she was taken from me?

I wouldn't survive it.

But I didn't want to live without her either.

I steered the Jeep in between two white lines and shifted it into park. I glanced out the windshield and did a double take. I hadn't planned on coming here. I left her standing at the front door, wearing those tight jeans and furry boots, and I went on autopilot.

I glanced at the sign in the window of the shop and laughed.

It was the kind of laugh that expelled some of my worry and replaced it with a lighter feeling—a feeling of rightness.

It was time I made more out of my life. I would forever mourn the men that died, but I couldn't act like I died too. I didn't. I was still here. I still had the opportunity to be one lucky bastard. Yeah, the thought of losing Honor scared the shit out of me.

But she was young. She was healthy. We weren't in a war zone. The odds were in our favor.

Except, of course, for one thing.

Lex.

He was a threat to me. To Honor.

I was trained to eliminate threats. Eliminating him would be a freaking pleasure.

I yanked the keys out of the engine and stepped out onto the pavement. I felt better now that I had some sort of plan.

But first, there was something I had to do.

29

Honor

I heard his Jeep crunching over the gravel in the driveway and my pulse immediately picked up. It'd been only hours since I saw Nathan last, but I missed him. He was never far from my mind the entire day.

My mother seemed to know it too. She kept giving me these knowing looks and asking coy questions about Nathan whenever she could work them into the conversation.

My father, of course, seemed oblivious to it all so I spent most of my time with him. I stayed through dinner and then drove home. I wanted to get here before dark... It gave me a chance to check all the closets and showers for anyone who might be lurking.

And yeah, I was totally anxious to see Nathan again.

Before he left, he said he'd be back tonight and he would take me to his place. Good Lord, his place. My body was still humming from what he did to me on that coffee table. But I was also hungry… hungry for more.

Part of me hoped we did very little sleeping in the king-sized bed he claimed to have.

I raced down the steps like an excited teenager barely able to contain my excitement when he knocked on the front door. Brisk air rushed inside and swirled around me when I pulled open the door, but I barely noticed the cold.

Nathan was standing there in a pair of loose-fitting jeans, boots, and a rust-colored T-shirt. Over top, he wore a grey fleece jacket that was zipped a little bit more than halfway. He'd shaved since I'd seen him last and his jaw was completely smooth.

"Hey," he said, grinning.

"Hi." I stepped back so he could come in and shut the door behind us.

"So, I did something," he said a little sheepishly.

After I locked the door, I gave him a funny glance. "What?" I couldn't help but notice the way he was standing with one arm sort of wrapped over his middle.

"I got you a present."

"You already gave me a gun."

He gave me a lopsided smile. "This is something you'll actually like."

I laughed. Something inside his jacket moved. "Ummm, please tell me there isn't an alien baby inside your stomach, trying to claw its way out."

He laughed. "Only a writer would think up something like that."

"Hey. It could happen." I said, still watching the lumpy movement beneath his coat.

Very gently, he reached into the inside of his jacket and withdrew my gift.

I gasped and stared at the little wiggly bundle in his palm. It was a puppy.

"You got me a puppy?" I said, staring at the fluffy little guy. The puppy couldn't have been more than two pounds.

"Life's short. No time like the present to get what you want," he said. I could hear a tiny bit of wariness in his tone. Giving someone a puppy was like the gift that kept on giving. Giving poop and pee on your rug.

"Can I hold him?" I cooed, reaching out for the tiny little body.

"It's a girl," he said, handing her over.

"She's precious," I whispered, cradling her against my chest. She was white with a few light tan spots on her back end and on her nose. One of the puppy's ears was tan and they both stood up and were bigger than her head, making her look like Dumbo, and they were fuzzy with long strands of ultra soft hair sticking out wildly around them.

I laughed and stroked her softness. "Hi," I told the puppy. It made a little puppy sound and my heart completely melted.

I wandered up the stairs, still holding her against me, and then sat down on the living room floor in the center of the carpet.

"It's a Chihuahua," Nathan said, coming into the room. "She's only eight weeks old. She was the runt of the litter and probably won't even grow to be five pounds."

"You're just a tiny little thing," I told her. She licked my chin.

I fell in love with her.

"She's really mine?" I said, looking over at him.

"I sure as hell hope you want her. Can you imagine me walking that tiny-ass dog on a leash?"

I laughed. "You mean you'd keep her if I said no?"

"Well, I sorta already spent the whole afternoon with her. She likes me."

The very fact that he was completely in love with this dog made her all the more appealing. "I'm gonna call her Lucy."

"Lucy, huh?"

"Got a better idea?"

"I've been calling her Killer."

I rolled my eyes. "This is not the face of a killer," I crooned to Lucy, holding her up so I could look into her tiny face. She licked me again.

"Lucy it is," Nathan said. "You're going to be one of those women that dresses that dog up in pink sweaters, aren't you?"

"She's going to need a coat," I said. "And a collar, a leash, food, toys…"

"There's food in the Jeep. I'll go get it."

While he was gone, I put Lucy down in between my spread legs, and she began to sniff me and the carpet. I couldn't stop petting her. She was so precious.

A few minutes later, Nathan came back and set a small bag of puppy food near the stairs. There was a pink, fuzzy baby blanket draped over his arm, and I lifted an eyebrow.

"She likes it," he said, shrugging.

Oh my God, he bought her a baby blanket.

I knew then that I was going to fall in love with Nathan Reed and nothing was going to stop it.

He stepped a little closer and Lucy's tail wagged as she made her way over to his feet. His feet looked like boats next to her miniature white body. He got down on the floor with her and she licked his nose.

"Are you sure you're going to let me have her?" I asked, watching him with the dog.

He nodded. "I plan to be around a lot, too."

"I could get used to that."

He leaned over and kissed me. Nothing else touched but our lips. We sat there in the center of the floor with Lucy between us, both leaning toward the other while our lips melted seamlessly together.

I would never get enough of kissing him. If he were the last person my lips ever touched, I would be amazingly happy.

Between us, little Lucy barked.

I laughed and pulled away to scoop her up. "Do you feel left out?" I asked, nuzzling her oversized ears.

"She probably needs to go out."

"I'll take her out in the backyard."

The lower level of my house was comprised of a laundry room and a family room that I used as my office. Inside the room, all my book covers hung on the wall in poster size; a bookshelf lined the far wall and was filled with my books and the books that I loved to read. Also there was a desk and cabinet where I kept all my swag (promotional items) and a small couch where sometimes I liked to curl up and read.

"Is this where you write?" Nathan asked, looking around with curiosity on his face.

"It's my office. I tend to sit at the kitchen table upstairs when I write. It's closer to the coffee." I slid open the sliding glass door and stepped out onto the very large piece of slate that was lying on the grass. I sat Lucy down and she sat there and looked up at me.

"Go pee," I told her. She just sat there. "Lucy!" I said excitedly. "Go do your business!"

She waddled out into the grass, sniffing everything she could. I watched her as she explored.

Nathan stepped outside and wrapped his arms around me from behind. "How's your ribs?"

"They hurt." They hurt almost constantly. It was actually really annoying. "I'm going to take another pain pill before bed."

"You should go inside. It's cold out here. I don't want you to catch pneumonia."

"You can keep me warm." I sighed and leaned into him a little bit more. Nathan pressed a kiss to the side of my head. "Thank you for Lucy. She's perfect."

"I wasn't sure what kind of dog you wanted, but when I saw her, I thought of you."

"I still can't believe you bought me a dog."

"Like I said, life's too short to deny yourself the stuff you truly want."

I turned in his embrace and wrapped my arms around his neck. "Does that go for *all* things I truly want?"

"And what do you want, Honor?"

"I want you."

He studied me closely for long moments. "Are you sure?"

"I've never been so sure."

"After what he did to you…" Nathan said, his voice taking on a hard edge. "I wouldn't blame you if you didn't even want me to touch you."

"I think I proved earlier that I like when you touch me."

He chuckled. "That was totally hot."

"I want more," I whispered, ducking my face into his neck. "I want you."

The muscles in his body contracted and he groaned. "You make it really hard for a guy to resist."

I pulled back and looked up at him. "You want to resist me?"

"Oh, hell no, I don't. But I want you to feel safe with me."

"I do feel safe with you. I've never felt safer."

He lowered his head to kiss me, but behind us Lucy started barking. I spun around and looked at her. She stood in the center of the small yard, looking at the privacy fence that separated my yard from the trail.

"Lucy," I called, thinking her little puppy barks were awfully cute and not intimidating at all.

She glanced at me but then turned back the fence. The wind ruffled the single tree in the yard and golden yellow leaves shook free and spiraled toward the ground. Lucy took off after one, romping on it when it hit the ground.

"C'mon, you silly thing," I called, laughing at her cuteness.

She didn't listen, of course, but continued to attack the leaf like it was some sort of menacing object.

Nathan released me and stepped out into the grass. "Lucy, come." He squatted down and she came running over to greet him.

"C'mon, Killer," he said and scooped her up. I took her from his arms and kissed her head.

"Lucy," I corrected.

He grunted and we went back inside, Nathan sliding the door shut behind us. "Did you write all those books?" he asked, motioning to my covers lining the walls. To date, I'd written ten novels. I was close to finishing one and then I was supposed to start another.

"Yeah."

"I'd make a pretty good cover model, don't you think?" he asked, striking a pose.

Actually, he would be great on a book cover. "I'll take it under advisement."

"Maybe you should just write an entire series about me," he said as we went up the stairs.

I made a choked sound. "And call it what? *Tales of an Egomaniac?*"

He laughed.

"You know," I said, putting Lucy down on the carpet, "I actually thought about writing about what happened to me."

He nodded thoughtfully.

"I could add in the part about the heroic Marine who shows up to save the day."

"You saved yourself, Honor," he corrected. "You managed to get that phone. You didn't give up hope. You fought like hell to get away from him. I just showed up to help."

"You didn't even know me. Yet you came."

"Baby, I would go anywhere for you. I would drop everything and come running."

"But you didn't know me," I insisted.

"It didn't matter."

I knew that he would have come regardless; he would have gone out there for anyone who was in trouble. I actually felt kind of lucky it was me.

Was that sick? Did I need therapy?

"What's the matter?" he asked, studying my face.

"Do you ever wonder," I asked, "why things happen? You know the saying: 'there's a reason for everything.' Do you believe that?"

"I didn't used to, but I'm starting to believe that now."

"I do too."

"So what's your reason, Honor?"

"I think the reason I was kidnapped, the reason my texts went through to you, is because I was meant to meet you. You're my reason, Nathan."

The look on his face was sort of priceless. A million emotions crossed over him all at once. Shock, wonder… joy.

"You sure make it hard," he said, his voice hoarse.

"Make what hard?"

"For me to keep my hands off you."

"So don't. I want them on me."

This strained look came across his face, almost like he was in pain. "But what he did to you…"

"Stop thinking about what he did to me." I didn't want to think about it either.

"It makes me so angry, Honor," he growled, clenching and unclenching his hands at his sides.

I finally understood the anger I always sensed that seemed to simmer inside him. He was still angry about what happened when he was deployed. He was angry at the lives his friends never got to live.

He couldn't do anything about that.

But I could let him do something about what happened to me.

I stepped forward, closing the distance between us, and laid a hand over his chest. Tipping my head back, I stared up into his conflicted yet longing-filled navy eyes. "You can make it go away," I whispered. "Your touch will completely erase all the times he touched me. Once you lay your hands on my skin, I won't be able to remember anyone but you."

He groaned and captured my face between his palms. Nathan held me firmly, keeping me utterly still while he had his way with my mouth. Heat pooled in my belly and the blood rushed from my head. Still holding me in place, he nipped and licked his way down my neck, lightly sucking the sensitive skin into his mouth. I moaned, my knees threatening to buckle, and he finally released me. His hands glided down the curves of my body and wound around until he was cupping my butt in his very capable palms.

He whispered my name as he picked me up, my legs automatically hooking around his tapered waist. His grip stayed on my butt, and I rocked against him, rubbing my swollen bud along his abdomen.

He took two steps back and came up against the wall, where he leaned his shoulder blades and fastened his skilled lips to my collar bone. I filled my hands with every inch of him I could hold. His pecs filled my palms and I took pleasure in squeezing them, pinching at his nipples through his T-shirt until they were rock-hard knobs.

A sound of desperation ripped from my throat when I tried to reach the hem of his shirt and was blocked by my legs tightly clasped around him.

Nathan pushed away from the wall, one hand cupping my bottom and the other splaying across the small of my back as he strode along the hallway. As he walked, he reclaimed my lips in a searing kiss. His mouth was insistent and demanding; there was a possessive ferocity in the way Nathan kissed.

I began to slide down his body because my legs were so wobbly that I couldn't keep them tightly around him. I was dangerously close to turning into a giant puddle of need.

I slipped a little lower and his arm slid around my ribs. I jerked at the sudden jolt of pain, and he quickly laid me across the mattress. "Damn, baby, did that hurt?"

I nodded. "Real bad," I said, my voice so deep I barely recognized it.

Nimble fingers caught the hem of my paisley print top and he bunched it up beneath my armpits. I wasn't wearing a bra today because the pressure of the straps hurt too much. Thankfully, my breasts weren't large and I didn't really need a bra.

Of course, right about now, I wish I had more for him to look at.

I dared a peek up at his face and saw the way he was staring down at me. There was a reverence in his gaze that made me feel powerful. It made me feel desired.

Slowly, he stretched out alongside me, feathering the tips of his fingers across my belly and dancing them up a little higher. His eyes darkened until they looked like midnight as he took in the swelled area and the splotched bruises.

"If I could take this away from you, I would," he murmured and then ducked low, sprinkling barely there kisses across my torso.

I moaned and arched up off the mattress. I was beyond feeling any twinges of pain. Desire for him was in the driver's seat and my body knew exactly what it wanted. I palmed the back of his head and guided him upward, past my ribs to the softly mounded peaks that awaited his attention.

He fastened his lips over the one closest to him, drawing in the hardened pebble and nipping at it with his teeth. An animalistic sound ripped from his throat as he took me just a little deeper into his mouth. I held his head there, silently begging for more sweet torture.

Nathan was a thorough lover and what he did to one breast, he did to the other. My entire body was boneless as he worked his magic over my flesh and my legs fell open and my legs twitched, like he was scratching an itch I never realized I had.

When my breasts were pink and slightly swollen from all the lavish attention, he began to work his way down, dragging his teeth along my hipbone and then sliding his tongue down the little indent where my leg met the apex of my thighs.

He pulled away only long enough to settle between my knees and stripped away everything I was wearing until I was completely naked lying against the sheets. "I've never in my entire life seen a sight that takes my breath away until now," he whispered, caressing the skin of my inner thighs and causing my toes to curl into the sheets.

Nathan dove into my moist heat like I was an all-you-can-eat buffet and he was starving. I lifted up off the mattress, crying out with the first flick of his tongue over my clitoris. He slid his arm beneath the small of my back and tilted my hips up off the mattress, giving his mouth even more exclusive access.

I couldn't help but move against his mouth, small little thrusts that slid his tongue along my inner folds with mind-blowing perfection. I felt the exploration of his finger, and I caught my bottom lip in my teeth, waiting for the feeling of him slipping inside. I didn't have to wait long as two thick fingers worked their way into my opening and slid inside my body.

Breath hissed between my teeth and all thought left my brain.

Sensation after sensation tingled through my body and the blood that pumped through my veins felt like it had caught fire. A fine blush broke out over my body, and I started murmuring incoherent words that didn't make sense at all.

"Honor, baby," Nathan whispered as he curled his fingers forward, scraping against the inner wall deep, deep inside me.

My entire body rippled with the orgasm that stole over my body. For very long, blissful seconds, everything fell away. There was nothing but the roaring pleasure that I felt in every single ounce of my body.

My mouth fell open in a soundless gesture and I collapsed against the bed, still quaking occasionally from the aftershocks of whatever the hell he just did to me.

God, I hoped he would do it again.

Nathan collapsed on the bed beside me, breathing heavily and letting out a little growl. "I almost came right there in my jeans."

That reminded me. He was still fully dressed.

I pushed up onto one elbow and stared down at him. "It's my turn."

Both his eyebrows rose up his forehead. "I'm all yours, sweetheart."

30

Nathan

I reminded myself to take it slow, that traveling the road to burying myself as deeply as I could in the center of her body was half the fun.

But the way she stared at me, her eyes looked like glittering blue diamonds. Her cheeks were flushed and her hands... *oh shit,* her hands were curious.

"Take it off," Honor rasped, tugging at my shirt.

I didn't look to see where it landed when I tossed it away from us. The bedroom was very dim. The light that filtered down the hallway spilled inside to give me just enough illumination to see every curve of her lithe body.

Honor's eager mouth fastened on my nipple, and I knotted my fingers into her hair, holding her closer, urging her to suck a little bit deeper. She did, and I groaned as my erection strained against the zipper of my jeans.

"I like this," she said, kissing down my USMC tattoo, tracing the letters with her lips and then nipping at the skin as she worked her way across my abs.

I'd had sex with many women, but this was the first time I'd ever been so far gone and still wearing my pants. Honor plunged her tongue in my belly button as her hand reached for the button on my jeans. She fumbled with it at first, but then it gave way and she didn't wait a single second before dipping her fingers into the waistband.

The second her touch brushed over the straining tip of my penis, I growled and my hips bucked up off the bed. Honor crawled down a little and used both hands to glide down the zipper and open my pants completely. I sprang out like an eager jack-in-the-box, and her eyes widened in surprise.

"No underwear?"

I felt myself smile. "The boys like to breathe."

She didn't touch me, which about drove me insane. I wanted her mouth and her hands all over my body, but I stayed patient as she worked the jeans down over my hips and then around my ankles. I helped her out by kicking the pants off the end of the bed.

Both of us were completely naked.

Honor's gaze fastened back on my throbbing cock and, as if fascinated by it, she wrapped both hands around the base. I groaned as one of her palms slid down to cup my balls. She kneaded them softly, rolling them around, causing them to shrink up and become tight with freaking want.

Using her nails, she scraped down the inside of my thighs, and I parted my legs just a little bit more because I wanted her to have all the access she desired.

My eyes rolled back in my head when her mouth closed over me and slid down. She deep throated me, all the way down, until I could feel my head brush against the back of her throat. I pulsed inside her, so completely turned on that black spots swam before my eyes.

She sucked me so deeply and so thoroughly that I forgot where I ended and she began. Occasionally, she would pull all the way back and wrap her lips around that ultra-sensitive ring at the top of my erection.

I would jerk and quiver, my entire body would stiffen with release, but then she would pull back, just enough to bring me back from the edge. I pushed up on one elbow, my eyes narrowed into fine slits, and watched the way she licked at me. It was like she couldn't get enough.

"Baby," I called, my voice hoarse and guttural. She glanced up, dragging her tongue right over the tip where a small bead of pre-cum had formed. *"Fuck."* It was a curse and a prayer. "Come up here before you kill me." I encircled her elbow with my hand and gently guided her so she straddled my lap.

The slick moisture of her core slid over my stomach and I growled.

She was all I could see. I had tunnel vision. I had selective sight. The only thing in this entire world was her. Her tight little body sat atop me like I was some crazed stallion and she was in complete control.

I fucking loved it.

I grabbed her hips and rocked her center against me. She moaned and went to topple over. I held her up, reaching between us and stroking my finger into her center. "I need my jeans," I told her.

She slid off me and stumbled around the end of the bed. My jeans came flying up and would have smacked me in the head had I not caught them. I chuckled as I yanked out the foil packs in the back pocket and the tossed aside the clothes.

Honor stared at the packets in my hand and then crawled up onto the bed, making her way up my body until she was straddling my legs.

I used my teeth to rip open the packet and she watched as I deftly rolled it on, so totally ready for her I was afraid I would explode the minute her heat wrapped around me.

To my surprise, she started to climb off me, to lie on her back. I caught her. "Come back here," I whispered and then positioned her back on top. "You get to drive." I didn't want to put her beneath me, not now, not after everything she'd been through. I wanted her to feel safe and in control.

Her eyes flashed down to mine and a little smile curved her lips.

"What are you going to do?" she asked, reaching down to pinch one of my nipples.

"I plan to be a very vocal and naughty backseat driver."

Honor positioned herself over me and held my eyes as she began to slide down. It was the single most thrilling experience I'd ever known.

About halfway down, she paused, panting a little, her eyes wide. I noted the set of her shoulders and the fact she wasn't quite as boneless as she was before.

"It's been a while," she said by way of explanation. "And there is nothing about you that's small."

"Define a while," I growled, hating the idea of any other man touching what was mine.

"Over a year."

The possessive animal in me liked that answer. A lot.

One of my hands reached up and cupped her breast, weighing it in my palm and caressing the tight nipple, and my other hand slid between us and began caressing the sweet spot in her center. She moaned and looked at me.

I smiled and then pulled my fingers away and delved it inside her alongside my penis.

"Oh," she said breathlessly as she swiveled around.

I pulled my hand away and gripped the sides of her hips, not asking her to do anything but stay where she was. But she was ready for more.

Inch by delicious inch, her body accepted me. She was so incredibly tight that every single flex, every single contraction her body made reverberated right into my bones. My body actually trembled with the lust sweeping through my bloodstream.

And then her hips hit mine.

Her body completely took me in and I was buried so deep within her that I swear I could feel her heartbeat. Ever so slowly, she began to rock. Back and forth... back and forth. It was agonizingly slow and tauntingly passionate.

"Nathan," she murmured, leaning over so our chests were plastered together. She took my lips in a gentle kiss and I seized her hips and reared up, hitting against her inner wall.

That single movement seemed to flip a switch inside her and she began to move. She rode me like I was a wild mustang and she was the only one who could tame me. Her hips grinded against me so hard that I began to sweat. Tension coiled in my gut, like an angry snake ready to strike. I knew my orgasm was going to destroy me… and I was going to love it.

Frantically, we moved against each other, the pace picking up with each stroke. Finally, Honor made a desperate noise and bore down on me. I grasped her hips to keep her from moving, and I sat up, clutching her around the waist. Her arms and legs wound around my back and she buried her face in the hollow of my neck.

I knew I needed to slow down. Her ribs were in no condition for this kind of activity. I gentled my hold around her waist and started to lower back down onto the mattress.

Honor tightened her arms and legs around me, lifting her head to pin me with a pleading stare. "Don't stop."

"Your ribs…"

"I don't care about my ribs." She pulled me closer and I went because the feel of her grinding against my lap was just way too much to resist.

We moved together, the lower halves of our bodies grinding in perfect rhythm until the friction was almost too much to bear.

"Nathan," she cried, her voice strained and pulled taut.

With one last thrust, I started pulsing inside her and then she toppled over the edge. Honor moaned and sank her teeth into my shoulder. A great shout ripped from the back of my throat as my release went on and on and on.

I hugged her close, trying not to crush her ribs but unable to gentle my hold. I couldn't let her go. She was mine.

I was keeping her.

An hour could have passed; I had no concept of time. When our hearts finally returned to normal and I felt like I could breathe, I peeled her off my chest and looked into her flushed and relaxed face.

"I'm so glad I didn't die that night," I whispered, the words ripping out of me from someplace so incredibly deep. They were painful to say, but in that pain there was joy. Joy that I was finally learning to feel something other than guilt about being alive.

She made a soft sound and her eyes turned into liquid pools. Her hands cupped my face and she rested her forehead against mine. "Thank you for coming home. I've been waiting for you forever."

She reached between us and picked up the dog tags I always wore but seldom ever noticed. I'd been wearing them for so long it was like they were just another part of my body.

I watched as she brought the twin silver tags up to her lips and press a kiss to each one. She replaced the tags against my chest and then cupped my face once more, this time to kiss my lips and tilt my head down so she could kiss the edge of the scar on my cheek.

Something inside me cracked.

The wall of isolation and despair that I so painstakingly built around my heart fractured and completely tumbled away.

31

Honor

Holy hot mama. I felt like a kid who caught Santa putting presents under the tree on Christmas Eve and realized the jolly man in red was actually real.

Nathan was *real*. He wasn't perfect. He was a man who had seen many hardships, a man who faced death and war. He was scarred (inside and out), and he would likely always battle with some sort of inner demons.

It's what made him so remarkable. There were some people like him that might collapse under the weight of all they carried. But he didn't. Yeah, I could see in his eyes and hear in his voice there were times he stumbled, but he kept getting up.

I didn't want a knight in shining armor. Knights with shining armor were posers. Everyone knew that the really good knights were the ones whose armor bore chinks and scratches from a battle they were strong enough to survive.

I was still collapsed across his chest and my body still trembled with the after effects of making love to him, when I heard a little ruff from beside the bed. I smiled and pushed myself off him to peek over the side of the mattress. Lucy wiggled her tail, her entire back end twisting with it.

I laughed and scooped her up to snuggle her against my chest. She licked my face and then wiggled free, climbing on top of Nathan's exposed chest. He opened his eyes and looked at the puppy and smiled.

Lucy plopped her butt down right in the center off him and looked at him expectantly. A chuckle rumbled from his throat and he reached up to scratch behind her oversized ears. I lay down beside him, scooting close to his side, and rested my cheek against his shoulder.

We lavished attention on Lucy and every so often, Nathan would turn and kiss my forehead. I'd never felt so content in all my life. I felt like I was exactly where I belonged, and I couldn't be more grateful that Nathan (and Lucy) came into my life.

It seemed silly to feel so much so fast. If this were a book, my reviewers would be screaming "insta-love" all over their reviews. But it didn't matter what anyone else thought, not really. No one else could tell me what was in my heart. Besides, I wouldn't be confessing my undying love for him anytime soon. I wasn't in a hurry for that. I wanted to take my time with Nathan. I wanted to know everything he wanted to share. I wanted to explore his body until I knew every single detail, and then I wanted to start all over again.

"You're awfully quiet over there," he said, running a hand up my back. "Where'd you go?"

"I haven't gone anywhere. I'm still here, with you."

"No regrets?" he murmured, grazing the very tips of his fingers down the center of my spine.

I pushed up, propping my chin on my forearm and staring into his face. "None."

Nathan lifted his head off the pillow and brushed his lips over mine gently. But it wasn't enough and the kiss deepened instantly, our tongues colliding in endless, consuming affection. He felt warm and moist. His lips glided against mine effortlessly, like they knew exactly where to go and how to extract the most pleasure from me with just the right amount of contact. I felt my fingers curl into his chest, and I made a small sound of pleasure. Feeling emboldened, I sucked his lower lip between my teeth and nibbled at it. He gripped my bare butt and shot sparks of electricity throughout my body.

"You better put those teeth away unless you want to start a fire," he murmured, pulling away.

"Maybe I do," I purred.

He groaned. "Don't tempt me. I don't want to hurt you. Your ribs are probably feeling what we just did. You breathing okay?"

How could I breathe when he left me breathless?

"I'm fine."

"It's probably time for your pain meds."

"Probably," I agreed, making no move to get out of bed.

"We're supposed to stay at my place tonight," he reminded me.

"I don't wanna get up."

"I have to work in the morning. My uniform is at my house."

The thought of seeing him in his uniform gave me a little motivation to get moving. "Fine," I sighed and sat up. My ribs protested and I bit back a wince.

Nathan made a knowing sound and placed Lucy in my lap. "Stay there," he instructed.

Lucy rolled onto her back, showing me her rounded belly, and I began scratching her as she wiggled all around.

After Nathan made a quick stop in the bathroom, I heard him out in the kitchen, and a few minutes later, he came back with a glass of water and my pills. He was also carrying a plate full of pie.

I grinned and took my pill as he shoveled the pie into his mouth. "We're almost out of pie," he said around a huge bite.

"Heaven forbid." I gasped and set the water on the nightstand. "I guess I'll have to go to the store tomorrow and stock up on pie supplies."

He paused. "What do you do all day long anyway?"

I snorted. "I'm a writer. *I write.*"

"I don't like the idea of you being home all day alone all the time."

"I'm not alone. I have Lucy now."

He grunted and stuck the fork with a bite of cinnamon-covered apple in my face. I took it and chewed while Lucy climbed up my chest, licking at my lips, trying to get a taste.

"I should go feed her," I said, getting up and opening the closet doors.

"We'll head to my place after."

I pulled on a pair of pink sweatpants with the word *Aeropostle* down the leg, a white T-shirt, and a grey hoodie. In the bathroom, I ran a brush through my tangled hair and pulled it up into a messy knot on the top of my head. I couldn't help but notice the way certain parts of my body tingled and how I felt slightly stretched and swollen in my panties.

Just thinking about that made me want him all over again.

Nathan came in the bathroom behind me, his jeans pulled on but still unbuttoned. He wasn't wearing a shirt and his dog tags dangled between his pecs. I turned from the counter and ran my hands up his sides and looped them around his neck. He gave me a quick kiss, then pulled away.

"Are you trying to seduce me?"

"Is it working?"

"Hell yeah, it is."

I grinned.

Lucy began barking from on top of the bed.

"Easy there, Killer," Nathan called, and I smacked him in the stomach and went to gather her up.

In the kitchen, I put out plastic bowls of food and fresh water and called Lucy to come eat.

She was standing at the sliders, staring out into the darkness. All the little hair on her back was raised into a line.

"Lucy?" I called, motioning to her food. "Come on, girl."

She growled, not pulling her attention away from the darkness. A little tingle of fear traveled down my neck. I peered out where she was watching and, of course, saw nothing but darkness.

Lucy growled again and then started barking her head off. For such a little puppy, her growl was surprisingly aggressive.

This creepy feeling of dread washed over me and images of being attacked and thrown into the hole assaulted me. I did my best to push them away, not wanting to scare myself more. Suddenly, Lucy fell quiet. I breathed a sigh of relief and squatted down beside her food again and called her over.

But she still wasn't paying attention to me. She was still staring out into the darkness. The house creaked a little with a gust of wind, and I laughed lightly. "It's just the wind, you silly girl."

Lucy cocked her head to the side like she was listening, all her attention still on the darkness. I sighed and stood up, stepping toward the puppy. She let out a low growl and then started barking some more.

"Lucy, no," I admonished, reaching down to pick her up.

I hated to tell her no, but she was creeping me out.

Just as I wrapped my arms around her and straightened, something struck the thick glass of the door and it splintered loudly. I shrieked and spun, watching as a huge crack climbed its way up the window.

I stumbled backward, opening my mouth to yell for Nathan, when the sound of a shot outside reverberated through the night. The bullet slammed into the already fractured glass and it shattered. I felt the heat of it as it whizzed past my cheek and pain bit into my thigh.

Something heavy and hard hit me from behind, tackling me to the ground and smothering me into the tile. Beneath me, Lucy barked and whined as shards of thick glass rained around the room.

The sound of crushing glass and the bullet slamming into a nearby wall echoed through the room, and I cringed.

"Stay down," Nathan murmured in my ear, using his body like a shield to protect me.

"He's out there," I said as my hands began to tremble. Lucy whined and licked my cheek.

"Good," Nathan growled as his muscles locked and rage simmered beneath his surface. He wrapped his arms around my middle and then half-crawled behind the set of cabinets lining the wall. I sucked in short gasps of breath, my ribs screaming in pain, and my palm where my stitches were throbbed.

Something else hurt too… but my mind was swimming. It was trying to formulate a plan, trying to come up with some sort of way to fight back. It was really hard to think when adrenaline pumped through your limbs at an overwhelming rate.

All I could think was, *He's going to throw you back into the hole.*

Nathan rolled off me and crouched low, helping me sit up. Lucy was trying to rush off (likely scared to death), and I was gripping her tiny body, trying to keep her still.

"Shh," I told her and went to stroke her white fur.

But it wasn't white anymore.

It was red.

I let out a sharp cry and Nathan looked down, a string of curse words flinging from his mouth. "My puppy," I cried, running my hands over her, trying to figure out where she was injured. Rage like no other consumed me.

It was one thing to come after me, but it was something else entirely to come after a defenseless baby animal. The anger shoved away the fear, and determination flooded my brain.

"Lucy," I murmured, my voice breaking.

Nathan had stilled and was looking down.

"What!" I cried. Frantically searching her. "Where is it?" I demanded.

"It's not her," he said, his voice flat.

"What?" I said, looking up. His eyes were glassy and far away. His skin had paled as he stared down... I followed his gaze...

The blood was mine.

There was a huge chunk of glass sticking out of the top of my thigh. Blood seeped through the fabric of my sweats and was oozing out around the glass where it punctured deeply into my skin.

All I could think was thank God it wasn't Lucy or Nathan.

As blood continued to pump out of the wound, sliding toward the floor, Nathan stared at it, paralyzed.

"Nathan," I said, but he didn't seem to hear me.

"I'm gonna get the medic, Prior," he said, his voice far away. "I'm not going to let you die."

Oh God. He was having some sort of flashback from the night his unit was attacked.

"Nathan!" I cried, taking his face between my hands and forcing his gaze away from my blood loss. "Nathan! It's Honor. I'm fine. It's just a cut. I'm going to be okay."

Nathan's eyes remained glassy and then he blinked. "Honor," he whispered.

I nodded. "It's me. I'm okay."

He swallowed and glanced back down at my leg.

"Don't look," I urged, pulling his face back up to mine.

"I… I'm sorry," he murmured.

My heart cracked. "Don't be sorry," I said, squeezing his face. "Everything's fine."

"Don't die," he said, his whispered words breaking.

"Look at me," I demanded, swallowing past the enormous lump that lodged in my throat. "I am *not* going to die. *No one* is dying tonight."

Something in him seemed to hear me because a change came over him. He gave a brisk nod and clarity resurfaced in his eyes. He pulled out his cell from the pocket of his jeans and handed it to me. "Get the cops here. Now."

While I dialed, he reached up into a nearby drawer and pulled out a bunch of kitchen towels. Leaving the glass lodged in my leg, he used one of the towels and tied it just above the wound as tight as he could.

I gritted my teeth while I hurriedly gave the operator the information and my address.

Another bullet slammed into what was left of the glass, and I screamed. Nathan gave a shout and dove on top of me again, hunching himself around me as even more glass blasted into the room.

I felt his body jerk, and I yelled his name.

The operator on the line was saying, "Miss! Miss!" but I couldn't reply, not yet. When no other shots were fired, Nathan pulled back and I saw the dozens of little cuts from his shoulders all the way to his wrists, and I wanted to scream.

"C'mon," he said, not even acknowledging the injuries as he pulled me up and once again shielded me as we ran from the room. In the living room, I assured the operator that we were alive and asked her to hurry.

"The police are on their way, ma'am," she said. "Stay on the line."

Like I had time to talk. I set the phone down on the coffee table, leaving the line open, and then placed Lucy on the floor between the couch and the coffee table. I grabbed my purse and dumped everything out, reaching for the gun and flipping off the safety.

The sound of more glass shattering had my muscles stiffening. This time it wasn't coming from the kitchen; it was coming from downstairs, in my office. The sliding glass doors.

He was coming inside.

Nathan rushed over to where his jacket hung on the railing and pulled a pistol out of his pocket and a knife out of his boot.

Then he tossed me the keys to his Jeep. "Take Lucy and get outside. Get into the Jeep and start it up."

"What about you?"

"I'll be right behind you," he said, a determined look on his face.

He was going to face Lex. He wanted me to go outside while he went and risked his life.

Not gonna happen.

"Nathan," I said, trying to reason with him. The sound of crunching glass broke off my words, and I knew Lex was in the house. I could hear him knocking things over downstairs in my office as he ripped apart my home.

"*Now,*" Nathan ordered and grabbed me.

Lucy pawed at my ankle, and I picked her up, cradling her close. I rushed toward the stairs with Nathan leading the way and hobbled down the steps, feeling the sticky ooze of blood all the way down to my ankle.

Just as we reached the landing, a shadow appeared on the wall at the bottom of the lower level of the stairs and Nathan reacted instantly, catapulting over the railing and launching himself down the stairwell at our attacker.

"Go!" he roared as I heard the men grunt as their bodies tangled and slid down the stairs.

I wrapped my hand around the handle of the front door. The sound of fists hitting flesh had me spinning around to watch Nathan go at it with Lex, who was dressed in dark clothing with a black cap on his head.

They were so close together, banging into walls, rolling over the ground, that I could barely make out who was who.

And then a gun went off.

32

Nathan

I felt the bullet plow into my skin. I felt the first fiery pain cut into my flesh. And then I shut it down.

No bullet was going to stop me handing this bastard his ass.

I stumbled backward when he plowed into my middle, jamming his fingers in the bullet hole. I bit back a cry and knocked away his hands as I slammed into the wall. He took off through the office door and I pushed up and went after him.

I heard Honor calling my name, but I kept running.

I wanted this guy out of our lives.

Seeing blood rush out of her leg like that almost sent me over the edge. Like a time machine, it transported me back... back to that night when men I loved died. When I was forced to shoot and kill to protect myself. I tried to protect Prior that night.

I failed.

I wasn't going to fail again.

I rushed over the glass, feeling it cut into the bare soles of my feet, but I kept running. It was dark out in the yard, but my eyes adjusted quickly and I saw Lex leaping over the fence, and I leveled my gun at him and shot off a couple rounds.

Weapons were my job. I didn't miss my target.

He let out a stark cry and toppled off the fence and hit the ground with a hard thud. With my weapon still drawn, I made my way over to his side, where he was squirming around like a damned pansy.

I kicked him.

I never said I was a nice guy.

He coughed and wheezed; blood spurted out of his mouth and spotted his chin.

There was something about that chin that didn't seem right…

I kicked the gun out of his hands, and he reached for it, but I stepped on his fingers and bent down. He was still writhing. My bullet hit him in the chest, and I could tell from the sound of his breathing that his lungs were filling with blood.

I should have felt some remorse.

I didn't.

I would likely be haunted with more nightmares, more sleepless nights, but in that moment, I didn't care. I didn't feel a thing. The bullet in my side didn't register. The glass in my feet didn't hurt. I didn't think about the cuts on my arms as I reached down and yanked away the hat pulled low over his face.

It wasn't Lex. It was someone I'd never seen before.

I stared down at the man, who began to laugh.

"Sucker," he wheezed.

I slammed the butt of the pistol into his temple and cut off his laugh. My heart hammered as I spun around, fear and worry for Honor filling my veins with ice.

I listened through the darkness for the sound of the Jeep's engine. For proof that she listened and made it to the car.

There was no sound of a rumbling engine.

There was no sound at all.

The night was unnaturally quiet.

"Honor!" I roared, increasing my speed and pressing a hand to the wound in my side. Fuck, bullet wounds hurt.

From somewhere in the house, I heard the sound of Lucy's bark.

And then a gun went off.

33

Honor

Nathan was shot.

I saw the blood gushing out of his side and running down his bare skin to pool at the waistband of his jeans.

Where the hell were the cops?

"Nathan!" I shouted when he pushed off the wall and ran after Lex. He was an idiot! He was shot!

If he died, I was going to make the paramedics revive him so I could kill him all over again. Forgetting all about my orders from Nathan, I rushed back up the stairs and shut Lucy in the bathroom. She whined as I moved back down the hall, but I didn't know what else to do with her. At least in there she would be safe.

I gripped the gun as I rush-limped down the stairs. I wasn't about to let Nathan fight my battles for me. He already took some glass to his arm and back and a bullet. But this was my battle. That man out there was my kidnapper. I wasn't going to let him control me. I wasn't going to let him make me cower in fear.

When my foot hit the very last step, a dark figure stepped around the corner. I gasped.

It was Lex.

I'd know that handsome yet sadistic face anywhere.

I glanced behind him into my destroyed office and looked for Nathan. Where was he? Did he pass out? Was he dead?

"He's not too bright, is he?" Lex said. Just the sound of his voice made my insides curdle like spoiled milk.

"What did you do to him!" I demanded.

Lex smiled. "Not a thing. I'm saving all my punishment for you."

I looked at my kidnapper again. He wasn't wearing all black like the man Nathan was fighting. Lex was dressed in jeans, running shoes, and a black NorthFace jacket. He wasn't wearing a hat at all.

He looked like he came from the grocery store or something.

My eyes widened when I realized what happened. He tricked us.

"How did you find someone sick enough to help you?" I asked, glancing behind him once more. Where was Nathan?

"I'm offended you think I'm sick," he mocked.

"Even if you kill me, you won't get away with this. The police have Mary's locket. They already know what you did to me."

His eyes narrowed. "Yes. I saw the news. Not to worry," he said, taking a step forward as I took one back. "By the time the cops get here, you'll be dead and I'll be long gone."

"I don't understand why you're doing this," I said, remembering the gun clutched in my hand.

"Who says I need a reason? Maybe I just do it because I like it."

For some reason, I glanced down. His crotch was hard. Talk about a guy with sick fantasies. I swung up the gun and aimed it at his head. He lashed out, smacking the glass in my leg and making me cry out and stumble.

Lex took advantage of my momentary rush of pain and slapped my wrist and yanked the gun out of my hand. I kicked him and then scrambled up the steps away from him.

(Yes, I am aware I now joined the ranks of stupid idiots who run UP the stairs when a killer is after them.)

He grabbed my ankle and my chin slammed into the step. I felt my lip split open, and the pungent taste of blood flooded my mouth. I groaned, rolling onto my back and kicking with my free leg. My foot connected with his face. He let go, and I scrambled across the landing and up the second set of stairs.

Lex was hot on my heels as I raced into the living room, desperately looking for something I could use to defend myself.

The contents of my purse were still spilled everywhere, and the cell phone was still lit up and open on the table. "Help me!" I screamed in the direction of the phone. "He has a gun!"

Lex jumped me from behind, and I fell under him, onto my stomach and crying out as the glass in my thigh was shoved even deeper into my leg. Pain screamed through my body and tears filled my eyes.

I couldn't seem to think past the pain.

Lex flipped me over and straddled me. I forgot about the pain as my hand closed over something lying on the floor and I brought it up and jammed it down into the top of his thigh.

Lex shouted as the pen buried itself into his leg. Then I picked up a pack of Tic Tacs and threw it at his head. (What? I had to use what was available.)

He knocked the mints away and then reached for the pen sticking out of his leg. I twisted beneath him and he fell sideways. We went rolling across the floor as I reached up and gouged my thumb into his eye socket.

He jerked away and I followed him, ripping *my* gun out of his hand.

"Please stop!" I cried. I knew he wouldn't, but I admit, I yelled it for the benefit of the operator on the other end of the phone line.

I wanted absolutely no doubt that what I was about to do was self-defense.

Lex grabbed onto my ankle and grinned up at me. I kicked him in the face and blood bloomed around his teeth. He looked like some funhouse clown that had gone mad.

With a single jerk, he sent me falling backward, landing on my back.

Inside the bathroom, Lucy barked and I could hear her clawing at the door, trying to get out.

"After you're dead," Lex said, crawling up my body. "I'm gonna screw your body before it turns cold."

I shot him.

The bullet slammed into his shoulder and he recoiled. I scrambled out from under him and stood.

"Honor!" Nathan screamed from downstairs, and my knees went weak with relief.

"I'm up here!" I yelled, my voice sounding more like a squeak.

Feet pounded on the stairs, and I moved to rush toward him. I wanted his arms around me. I wanted to see that he was okay.

A hand closed around my ankle and jerked me back.

I screamed.

Lex laughed.

Twisting quickly, without hesitation, I shot him in the head.

Nathan skidded to a stop at the top of the stairs, his wide eyes going between Lex and me. I could only imagine what he saw. Me covered in blood with a busted lip and a heaving chest, holding a gun, while standing over a man with a bullet in his head.

Reality crashed over me.

The gun fell from my hand and bounced off the carpet.

I shot someone.

I killed him.

My kidnapper was dead.

"Honor," Nathan said breathlessly and rushed across the room to wrap me in his arms. My body shook violently, so hard that my teeth chattered and my skin felt icy.

"I killed him," I said, shoving my face into his bare, blood-smeared chest.

"You protected yourself, baby," he murmured. "You did real good."

Police sirens drew closer and soon, the flashing blue-and-red lights filled the windows and the driveway.

I felt lightheaded and I knew I lost a lot of blood. I pulled back from Nathan and looked at his side where the bullet entered his body.

"It's not so bad," he murmured, tipping my chin up so I couldn't look.

"He was crazy," I said, my voice hollow.

"Hell yes, he was." Nathan agreed, swiping the pad of his thumb across my chin. My lower lip was swollen again.

The cops burst in the front door with weapons drawn. I weaved a little on my feet. Standing up was growing harder and harder.

Nathan scooped me up in his arms and turned toward the cops. "I need a medic!" he roared.

Then he glanced down into my face. "Just hang on, Honor." He got this pinched look in his eyes. "Don't you die on me."

I smiled. "I wouldn't dream of dying. I have way too much to live for."

As my house filled with emergency workers and medical personnel, Nathan and I held each other's gaze.

"Me too," he murmured, pressing his lips to my forehead. "Me too."

EPILOGUE

Honor

One Year Later...

Flashbulbs exploded everywhere around us, blinding me, and I tried not to recoil. This night had been everything that dreams are made of, but all the attention, the crowds, and the noise was starting to wear on me.

Nathan wrapped a solid hand around mine and pulled me through the crowd toward the waiting limo. He held the door while I slid across the black leather seats, and he followed me in, shutting the door behind us.

"Holy cow," I gasped. "That was awesome and insane all at the same time!"

"Better get used to it. You're a celebrity now."

"I think you're more popular than I am." I smiled coyly from my side of the very long seat.

Nathan grinned and pushed off the door, slipping right up alongside me so we were pressed together, hip to ankle. "It's only because this author I know wrote this book about me that made me look like a real hero."

I climbed into his lap. The red gown I was wearing made it hard to move so I bunched it up around my thighs. "All I did was tell our story."

"You did more than that," he said, pride filling his voice. "You gave a voice to every single victim out there."

I wasn't so sure about that, but I did pray that I gave hope to some. Once the questioning, the media frenzy, and the funeral of Mary (her body was found weeks later, disposed in a crude shallow grave on the mountain) was over, Nathan and I settled into life together.

Being with him was more than I could have ever asked for. He made me so incredibly happy that I couldn't begin to regret being kidnapped.

But it wasn't something I was able to get over so quickly either. Nightmares, visions of Lex with a bullet wound in his head, and anxiety were all side effects of what happened.

Through it all, Nathan was there. He understood better than most people could. He never pushed, but his quiet strength was always there. He never complained when my screaming woke him in the night, and he put all his guns out of sight until I could look at one without feeling panic claw at my lungs.

I might have been the one to write a book about what happened to me, a book that debuted on the *New York Times* bestseller list and remained there to this day. I might have been the one whose name flashed in the credits on the big screen after the movie that was based on my book—*based on us*—

premiered tonight. But Nathan was the one who encouraged me to write it.

After watching me go through various stages of anger and guilt, he suggested I write it all down. That I sit and type out how I was kidnapped, what it was like to be in that hole. He told me that even if the book never saw the light of day, it could be a means of healing for me, a way to move on.

And so I did.

I wrote about everything. I wrote about Lex and the things he did to me. I wrote about the fear and loneliness that threatened to drag me down as I sat in that hole and stared up at the faraway sky. I told Mary's story, and I gave a voice to the family that would forever mourn her. But the book wasn't just about that. It was also a romance. It was the story of Nathan and me. It was the story of how love bloomed from a terrible thing and how it prevailed to this day.

The war veteran and the writer, both survivors, both getting the happy ending they deserved.

"I love you, Mrs. Reed," Nathan murmured, kissing my lips.

"I love you, too."

His palm slid up between us and covered my breast. I groaned and arched into his touch. We had made love about a thousand times in the past year, and I would never get tired of his touch, his feel, his scent.

"Can we skip the premiere party and go back to the hotel?" he said against my lips as his fingers rubbed over my hardened nipple.

I moaned. "I wish."

He pulled his lips away and leaned his head against the seat. "A bestselling book, a movie deal, a press tour…" he listed. "What's next?"

"Well," I said, fingering the ornate buttons on the Dress Blues he wore. "I was thinking we could buy a little place on the beach."

"Near Jacksonville?" he asked, his eyes lighting with interest.

"Your hometown." I smiled. "Think Lucy will like the beach?"

He chuckled. "What will your mother say?"

"Oh, I'm sure she'll call and bug us twenty times a day."

"Patton called me the other day. He's getting out of the Corps. I told him my idea about opening up a security firm."

"What did he say?" I said, excitement for Nathan unfurling in my belly.

"He said he wanted in." Nathan grinned like the cat that ate the canary.

"Of course he did," I replied, sliding my hands up his shoulders. "New house, new place, new business."

"I kind of always thought I'd do my twenty in the Corps and then spend my life alone. Yeah, I have my family in Jacksonville, but I didn't think I'd have a family of my own."

I folded his hand in mine. "Do you regret getting out of the Marines?"

He turned thoughtful and then he smiled. "No. That wasn't the kind of life I wanted. Not anymore. Not for me. Not for you."

"Life's too short to not get what you want," I told him, remembering when he said those words to me as he gave me Lucy.

"Exactly," he murmured, cupping my face in his palms. "It's a good thing I have everything I could ever ask for sitting right here in my lap."

One text is what started it all.

A single text led us to forever.

One text can change everything.

The End

Nathan's Apple Pie

Ingredients
**You can use store-bought crust or you can make
your own.**
To make a double pie crust:
2 2/3 cups all-purpose flour
1 teaspoon salt
½ cup butter
½ cup shortening
6 tablespoons ice-cold water

Apple Pie Filling:
4-8 Granny Smith apples (depends on size)
4 tablespoons cut-up butter
½ cup granulated sugar
2 tablespoons ground cinnamon (Nathan likes lots of
cinnamon. This can easily be cut down to taste.)
1 tablespoon all-purpose flour (This helps the sauce
in the pie thicken.)

Nathan's Apple Pie (cont.)

Directions
To make crust:

Cut together the flour, salt, butter, and shortening with a pastry fork until blended. Add water one Tbsp at a time and mix with fork until it firms into a ball. Separate the ball into two smaller balls. Roll each out onto a heavily floured surface, flipping over frequently. Place one crust in the bottom of a pie pan and reserve the other crust for topping the pie once it is full.

To make filling:

Peel and slice all the apples. Add all slices into a bowl. Mix the apples with the sugar, cinnamon, and flour until well coated. Dump apples into pie crust. Place the 4 tablespoons of cut-up butter around on top of the apples.

Cover the pie with the remaining crust. Crimp the edges together. With a sharp knife, cut a few slits in the top crust (to allow steam to escape while baking), and then you can brush the top of the pie with an egg wash (egg wash = a beaten raw egg). This will give the crust its golden-brown appearance. Also, sprinkle granulated sugar over the top of the crust—which will give the pie a nice flavor and sweetness.

Bake the pie in an oven preheated to 400 degrees for 40-50 minutes, depending on oven.

Let cool and enjoy!

Note: Nathan suggests serving your warm apple pie with a generous helping of French vanilla ice cream. Cambria recommends enjoying with ice cream AND coffee.

TIPSY

Sneak Peek

Julie
How they met...

Morning from hell. I was not a morning person. I never was, and I never would be. Getting up in the morning is pretty much the worst part of my day. Trying to drag myself out of a way comfortable bed where I am surrounded by fluffy pillows and soft bedding is pretty much the epitome of torture.

Add an alarm that never shuts up and cold tile in the bathroom that feels like tiny needles being jammed into my skin and you have the makings for a very bitchy Julie.

Thank goodness I lived alone. There was no way in hell any man could go up against the morning sunshine I projected.

To make matters worse, I was running late. I hated being late. If I was late to work, it would throw off every appointment I had that day, and I would spend every single hour trying to play catch-up.

I rushed around trying to get ready, pulling on a cotton dress because it was a hell of a lot harder to try and match clothes together when I was stumbling around like a living zombie (Wait. Zombies didn't live. They were dead.) and then buckled a red patent leather belt around my waist on the way down the stairs. I would have to do my eye makeup at work and I would also have to touch up my hair.

Glancing at the clock, I sighed and gave a longing glance at my kitchen where the coffee was kept.

I didn't have time for caffeine. I felt sorry for everyone who had to deal with me today.

I grabbed my purse and rushed out the door and climbed into my little silver car. The air was already thick, and I knew soon, the summer heat was going to bear down on this town like a hungry woman at Waffle House.

I turned out of my neighborhood and tore down the street, letting out an unladylike curse when I got caught by a red light.

When it turned green, I sped around the corner and glanced at the clock. Five minutes.

Flashing blue lights had me glancing in the rearview mirror. More unladylike curses exploded from my mouth as I pulled to the side of the road and prayed the cop would speed by.

Of course he didn't.

He pulled to a stop behind me.

I so did not have time for this.

Why is it that police officers always pick on the innocent people who rarely ever speed, yet they never pull over the people who are complete assholes on the road all the time?

Maybe I would ask him.

He knocked on the window and I sighed. I wasn't even going try to talk my way out of this one. It would be safer if I kept my mouth shut. It certainly would be cheaper.

I pressed the button and my window rolled down.

"License and registration, please," said a voice from above.

I let out another huffing sigh and leaned over, digging around in my bag and glove compartment for the items, and thrust them out the window while staring straight ahead. I could practically feel all the other drivers laughing at me as they drove past.

It really didn't improve my caffeine-deprived mood.

A few minutes later, the police officer leaned down in the window. "Did you know you were violating the speed laws, ma'am?"

Forget being quiet. I couldn't do it. I turned my head and opened my lips to give him a less-than-polite answer.

Every single word fled my brain. I mean, my vocabulary literally ran away. I couldn't even blame it. There was no word that could compete with such a face.

His eyes were such a deep blue that they held me captive in a single glance. He had a masculine and angular face, with a straight nose, full lips, and a cleft in the center of his chin. He was clean shaven and smelled so good that I actually leaned closer.

Who in the hell actually leaned closer to an officer who wanted to give her a speeding ticket?

He was lean, but not too thin, tall, and did his uniform justice. I was a little embarrassed to admit the gun strapped to his hip turned me on.

And then I saw the handcuffs.

I didn't know I was a dirty ho until that moment. I imagined all kind of inappropriate things that would involve those handcuffs.

He took off his hat and ran his hand through his hair. "Ma'am?"

I glanced at him, once again struck by his eyes. I felt the need to lean even closer, but I stopped myself.

"What?" I said, the word coming out a little harsher than I intended.

I swear he stifled a smile. "You were speeding..." he said, trailing away.

I couldn't stop staring at the little dent in his chin. My tongue would fit in it perfectly. I cleared my throat. "I'm late for work." The statement brought me back to reality. "Shit!" I yelled, hitting the steering wheel. "I'm late for work."

I winced and turned back to him. "Are you going to arrest me now?"

He laughed. He actually threw his head back and laughed.

God, he was sexy.

"Where do you work?"

"Right up the street at Razor's Edge Salon."

"You make a habit of speeding through an intersection?"

I made a frustrated sound. "Only on days I don't get my coffee, have to get out of bed at ungodly hours, and..." Oh, crap, there I went again. I looked at him meekly. "No?"

"No coffee, huh?"

"No," I grumped.

He sighed and straightened. He pulled a pad out of his pocket and then proceeded to write on it. I wondered how much this was going to cost me.

A minute later, he handed me back my ID and registration. I put them away and turned back to collect my sentence.

He put the notepad back in his pocket.

"Isn't that for me?"

He leaned back down in the window, bracing his forearms on the side of the car. "Nope. It's for me."

I felt my forehead crease. "I know I'm not properly caffeinated, but don't people who speed usually get tickets?"

"Usually," he agreed.

I lifted my eyebrows. I was back to being unable to speak. He was incredibly close.

"I'm going to let you off with a warning this time."

I made a sound that might have broadcast like an agreement.

He grinned. "On one condition."

I scowled. "I read an article about this once. Officers of the law letting people go in exchange for… *favors.*"

He chuckled. "Is that so?"

I crossed my arms over my chest. "I'm not that kind of girl, Officer Shady."

He lifted an eyebrow, and I felt my cheeks heat. *That's good, Julie. Insult a cop.*

"Are you the kind of girl who would go on a date with a shady police officer?"

My hands broke out in a clammy sweat. *Did he just ask me out?* "That depends," I said saucily.

What the hell is wrong with me this morning?

At the rate my day was going, I was going to shave off someone's eyebrow and turn their hair green.

"On?"

"How many times this admitted shady cop has pulled women over to ask them out on dates."

He flashed a smile and my heart stuttered. "Never."

I wasn't sure I believed that, but I wanted to. "If I agree, will you let me go to work?"

"Yep."

"Okay, then."

He smiled again and straightened, putting on his hat. "Watch your speed," he said, tapping the side of my door with his fingers.

"Don't you want my number?"

He leaned down once more. "Already got it. What do you think I was writing down?"

"I'm pretty sure that's abuse of your job."

He chuckled. "You gonna call my boss and rat me out?"

Hell no, I wasn't. "Maybe."

"I don't think so," he said softly.

"What makes you so sure?"

"Because, Julie," he drawled, and I swear my name on his lips made me lightheaded, "you want to go out with me."

I did. But I wasn't going to tell him that. He was already suffering from an oversized ego. "You gong tell me your name?"

"Blue," he said, stepping back from my car.

I'd never heard that name before. But considering the pull of his eyes, I understood it.

"Well, Blue, I guess I'll see ya when I see ya."

"Oh, you'll see me. Tonight. I'll pick you up at six."

Tonight? He worked fast. Maybe he should get a speeding ticket.

I waited until he was in his cruiser before I pulled out onto the road. He pulled out behind me and followed my car the entire way to the salon. When I pulled in the lot, he kept going, and I blew out a nervous breath.

I needed to revise my earlier statement. It was no longer the morning from hell.

For once, I was actually glad I got my ass of bed.

Ready for more of Julie and Blue?
Download and read **TIPSY** in full,
December 2013!

ACKNOWLEDGEMENTS

This book was like a little whirlwind in my life.
Let me tell you about that. Oh, and I was thinking…
maybe I shouldn't be calling this section the
acknowledgements… maybe I should be calling it a
"Note from the Author" because I do more babbling
about the book and what I was doing when I wrote it
than I do actually acknowledging people. Besides, I
thank the same people over and over again… Y'all
know who I'm gonna thank by now. Tweet me at
@cambriahebert and tell me what you think!

Okay, anyway, back to my story. *TIPSY* was
supposed to be the book published in November of
this year. I was going on with writing Julie and Blue's
story and I kept getting distracted. I kept losing focus.
The people in my head would not be quiet. The
loudest of them all was Honor. This girl had a story
and she wanted to tell it. Now. And Nathan… Well,
Nathan really wanted some pie.

So… I put *TIPSY* on hold to just start *TEXT*,
just to give Honor her voice. Once I started writing, I
couldn't stop. This book literally poured out of me.
The more I wrote, the more special it became. I
thought about Nathan all the time. Oh, and by the
way, Nathan is named after my son.

I think this book has a lot of similarities to my
own life. It kind of turned into a personal story for
me. Before you go gasping, NO, I have not been
kidnapped and thrown into a hole. But I do have a
very active imagination, and this is actually something
I used to fear.

My husband is a Marine. He was stationed in
Allentown like Nathan. Honor's house was the one

that we lived in when we were stationed in Pennsylvania. I used to walk on the Slatington Trail almost every day. Our house sat on the trail just like Honor's did. I ran on the trail one morning alone. I got about a mile into my run and realized that I could be kidnapped at any moment and no one would know. I spent the rest of my run trying not to pee my pants and peering into the heavy trees and bushes that lined the path.

True story.

I never ran alone again. I did walk with my dogs and kids and my husband. It is an absolutely gorgeous area. The roads are narrow and curvy. I got carsick every time we went somewhere for like the first month we lived there. One time we went to Wal-Mart using the GPS to give us directions… It took us over a mountain (like the one Nathan drives up to find Honor) and there was literally a sign that said, "Drive at your own risk."

I stopped shopping at Wal-Mart when we lived there. Ha ha hahahaha.

Honor is a writer like me. So I could identify with that as well. I also have a little dog that is the love of my life. I wanted to name her Lucy. My daughter wanted to name her Cocoa. Her name is Cocoa. LOL. But that's okay. It fits her really well.

So I guess really what I'm getting at is that this book is sort of born of my own life. The location, the house, Nathan's profession (a Marine), and Honor's profession, the dog, the trail… writing about it all came naturally to me.

Oh, and I really like apple pie.

The homemade piecrust recipe that I put in the back is actually my great grandmother's recipe. It's a family recipe. My mom makes it really good. I'm like the worst pie crust maker ever. I can bake, but pie crust is not my thing. I always buy it. Ha ha. While I was writing this book, I made two apple pies all because of Nathan.

So that's how this book came about. I really hope you enjoy it as much as I do. The cover, the story… it really became a love affair for me. I hope it does well out there in the world.

I would like to acknowledge Regina Wamba for creating this cover. It is my favorite cover to date. Something about it just speaks to me. Thank you, Regina, for making it and for putting up with my crazy messages about how much I love it.

I'd like to thank the model, Matt Hansen, who is pictured on the cover. Matt, you're hot. And you take an awesome cover photo.

To Cassie McCown, my personal book doctor, who whipped this book into shape, got rid of all my gibberish (and let me tell you, some of the sentences I wrote made no sense), and polished up the story the way it deserved. You're a great editor and I love working with you.

To Sharon Kay, my formatter. Thank you for always getting the formatting done in a timely manner. Thank you for making the inside of the books look as great as the outside.

I'm a lucky girl to have such a great team of people around me.

Of course, thank you to my family. My husband, who answered all my military questions and to my kids, who let me work when I needed to.

Finally, to all YOU, the readers, the fans… I wouldn't be able to keep publishing and writing if you weren't there to read it and support me. I'll be forever grateful.

Now, if you will excuse me, I have to get back to writing *TIPSY*. Julie and Blue have been very patient.

Cambria Hebert is the author of the young adult paranormal *Heven and Hell* series, the new adult *Death Escorts* series, and the new adult *Take it Off* series. She loves a caramel latte, hates math, and is afraid of chickens (yes, chickens). She went to college for a bachelor's degree, couldn't pick a major, and ended up with a degree in cosmetology. So rest assured her characters will always have good hair. She currently lives in North Carolina with her husband and children (both human and furry), where she is plotting her next book. You can find out more about Cambria and her work by visiting http://www.cambriahebert.com.

"Like" her on Facebook:
https://www.facebook.com/pages/Cambria-Hebert/128278117253138
Follow her on Twitter: https://twitter.com/cambriahebert
Pinterest: https://pinterest.com/cambriahebert/pins/
GoodReads:
http://www.goodreads.com/author/show/5298677.Cambria_Hebert
Cambria's website: http://www.cambriahebert.com

ALSO CHECK OUT THESE EXTRAORDINARY AUTHORS & BOOKS:

Alivia Anders ~ Illumine
Cambria Hebert ~ Death Escorts Series (Recalled & Charmed)
Angela Orlowski Peart ~ Forged by Greed
Julia Crane ~ Freak of Nature
J.A. Huss ~ Tragic
Cameo Renae ~ Hidden Wings
A.J. Bennett ~ Now or Never
Tabatha Vargo ~ Playing Patience
Beth Balmanno ~ Set in Stone
Lizzy Ford ~ Zoey Rogue
Ella James ~ Selling Scarlett
Tara West ~ Visions of the Witch
Heidi McLaughlin ~ Forever Your Girl
Melissa Andrea ~ The Edge of Darkness
Komal Kant ~ Falling for Hadie
Melissa Pearl ~ Golden Blood
Alexia Purdy ~ Breathe Me
L.P. Dover ~ Love's Second Chance
Sarah M. Ross ~ Inhale, Exhale
Brina Courtney ~ Reveal
Amber Garza ~ Tripping Me Up
Anna Cruise ~ Maverick

Text

Cambria Hebert

CPSIA information can be obtained at www.ICGtesting.com
Printed in the USA
LVOW08s1036131113

361147LV00004B/132/P